Alan Perry is a poet, painter and short story writer living and working in Swansea. A past winner of the Eric Gregory Award for Poetry, he has edited (or co-edited) all eight issues of *Cheval* and recently edited the Welsh section of *When young Dodos meet young Dragons*, an anthology of Welsh and Mauritian writers under the age of thirty-five, which was published in Mauritius and launched jointly there and in Wales. He has been married to painter and portraitist Jean Perry for fifty years and they have two sons who are also artists.

Jonathan Edwards' first collection, *My Family and Other Superheroes* (Seren), won the Costa Poetry Award 2014. It was shortlisted for the Fenton Aldeburgh First Collection Prize and the Wales Book of the Year. He won the Terry Hetherington Award in 2010 and received a Literature Wales New Writer's Bursary in 2011. His poems have won prizes in the Cardiff International Poetry Competition, the Ledbury Festival International Poetry Competition and the Basil Bunting Award, and have appeared in magazines including *Poetry Review*, *Poetry Wales*, *New Welsh Review* and *The North*. He works as a teacher.

CHEVAL 8

Edited by Alan Perry
and Jonathan Edwards

Foreword by Aida Birch

Parthian, Cardigan, SA43 1ED
www.parthianbooks.com
ISBN 978-1-910901-03-8
First published in 2015 © the contributors
Edited by Alan Perry and Jonathan Edwards
Cover design by Alan Perry
Cover painting by Jean Perry: 'MORWENNA'
(2015, watercolour on paper, 14x12", collection of the artist)
Typeset by Head & Heart Publishing Services
Printed and bound by Gwasg Gomer, Llandysul, Wales

CONTENTS

Review of Cheval 7 by Éadaoín Lynch   xi
Foreword   xv
Preface   xix
Acknowledgements   xxiii

Terry Hetherington
'The Gift'   1
'Movement'   2

Emily Blewitt
'How to Explain *Hiraeth* to an Englishman'   3
'Pisces Rising'   5
'The Philobrutist'   7

Aimee Bray (Highly Commended)
'Persephone's Underworld'   9

Eleanor Butler
'Economical'   16

Jenni Derrick
'On the Pier'   20
'The Happy Man'   21

Tom Gatehouse
'The Other Tower'   22
'Windmills of Groningen'   30
'Concerning an Unlikely Femme Fatale'   31
'Urban Villanelle'   32

Eluned Gramich (Third Prize)
'Rossiya'   33

Natalie Ann Holborow (First Prize)
'Blood Sugar'   44
'Bite'   46
'Vinegar'   50

Claire Houguez (Highly Commended)
'Within the Yellow Plumage'   59

Lucy Ann Jones (Commended)
'Table Set for Two'   68
'The Parade'   69
'The Voyage Out'   71

Richard Lewis (Second Prize)
'Work in Progress'   75
'23.57'   77
'Some News'   78

Lowri Llewelyn-Astley (Highly Commended)
'Melon'   80

Nicole Payan (Commended)
'Sweet Peas'   85

Whyt Pugh
'The Big Send Off'   91

David Schönthal
'Cairn'   102

Luke Smith
'No More Bets Please'   110

Daniel Williams
'Thinking in English'   119
'Taking Place'   121

Jessica Winterton
'The Oozlum Bird'   123

Liz Wride (Commended)
'Welsh Dragons'   132

New work from previous winners and commended
entrants in the Terry Hetherington Award

Glyn Edwards
'Wuthering Heights'   145
'L'Accalmie (Baie Saint-Paul)'   146

Grace Gay
'The Company of Pigeons'   148
'Birmingham Underpass'   149

Molly Jamieson
'Melissa the Magnificent'   151

Tyler Keevil
'Fishhook'   156

Anna Lewis
'Boxing Day Matinée'   164

Joâo Morais
'The Forage'   171

Thomas Morris
'The First Time I Met My Father'   178
'Frail Deeds'   182

Mao Oliver-Semenov
'What's outside the box?'   187

Siôn Tomos Owen
'God Bless 'merica'   188

Gareth Smith
'Desperation'   198

Katherine Stansfield
'The girls on the train'   209

Rose Widlake
'17'   210

Georgia Carys Williams
'The Giving'   213
'Succubus Speaks'   215

Terry Hetherington
'Feathering'   216
'In Memory'   217

Notes On Contributors   220

Also available

Cheval 7

Cheval 6

Cheval 5

Cheval 4

Cheval 3

Cheval 2

Cheval

REVIEW OF *CHEVAL 7*
FROM *NEW WELSH REVIEW*

Cheval, the publication for winning entrants to the Terry Hetherington Young Writers' Award, produced its seventh anthology last year. Its aim, 'to provide a platform for young people to express themselves through the medium of poetry and prose', lives on as a dedication to the late Terry Hetherington, whose ethos was of encouragement and support. Hetherington was a creative writing teacher and a significant source of comfort and assistance for young Welsh writers.

Entries are arranged alphabetically according to the author's surname, with the exception of the dedicatory poem to Terry Hetherington, Nigel Jenkins' 'Some Lines to Request Poteen', and four poems by Hetherington himself which bookend the anthology. Welsh references abound in each piece within the collection, particularly the three winning entries, Robin Ganderton's 'And So We Beat On,' Siôn Tomos Owen's 'Every Cloud,' and Georgia Carys Williams' 'Turnstones.'

Ganderton's short story took first prize for the award, having deftly utilised the difficult form of vignettes, and in less than ten pages offers a tender insight into his characters, such as 'We cannot believe, we will not believe, and we do not believe until one pale yellow day in early April, with sunbeams raking the carpet, when he picks up his Tanglewood and slowly, hesitatingly, begins to pick out a tune.'

The first poem of the collection, Maria Apichella's 'Fire,' displays a thorough understanding of the intensity of the lyric form, with its powerful last line, 'My prayer will burn for days.' Emily Blewitt's 'Noir', a poem that was highly commended for the award, illustrates a progressive use of mythology mixed in with modern life: 'I have wanted the killer-blow:/my femme fatale, her smile glowing.../Thin, expensive cigarettes/lit by someone, somewhere else.'

Tom Gatehouse's short story, 'Portuguese Lesson: O Acidente,' fuses English and Portuguese seamlessly. His accompanying poem, a villanelle, demonstrates his dexterity and confidence. Similarly, Natalie Ann Holborow's 'London' is an astonishingly vivid poem, capturing the essence of the British capital, with 'cindered veins,' 'Primrose Hill, rolled wide by the fog,' and 'slack-jawed Highgate.' In addition, Luke Smith's story, 'From Cambridge to King's Cross,' illustrates a self-consciousness that conceals the youth of its author. The internal monologue form interspersed with the main character's own prose writing within the story represents the high standard of writing and willingness to experiment that can be seen throughout *Cheval 7*.

The last seventy pages are devoted to previous winners and commended entrants' new work, notably Glyn Edwards' 'The Grave of a Ground,' which requires the reader to fold out the page and read the literally, and significantly, cross-shaped poem and its powerful use of language: 'Outside the club is an ashen mound. A handful/ of black sawdust, weightless and portentous./A coffin is not as heavy as a death.'

The experiments with form in both prose and poetry highlight the considerable abilities of the Welsh writers published here. As Aida Birch outlines in the Foreword, 'The

2014 Terry Hetherington Young Writers' Award brought the judges of the competition a very hard task indeed. The submissions have all been particularly praiseworthy.' Many of the works published here read as though written by established authors, displaying a confidence in tone, content and form that belies their experience.

As represented on *Cheval's* striking front cover (by David Perry), 2014 had a special significance as the centenary of Dylan Thomas' birth and the beginning of World War One. As such, Jonathan Edwards outlines in the preface, '2014 is the year of looking backwards.' But Cheval 7 is 'a book… that looks relentlessly forward.' The talent of its writers promises a great deal in the future.

Éadaoín Lynch, from NWR issue 107
Buy the book at gwales.com

FOREWORD

The Terry Hetherington Young Writers' Award is not only an award that offers opportunity to young writers, many writers wish to remain involved.

The winner of the 2015 award, Natalie Ann Holborow, submitted a powerful poem, 'Blood Sugar.' She allows the words to flow free from the heart. She remembers spending Christmas in hospital. She was diagnosed as suffering from diabetes at a young age. The wards, decorated with tinsel, were, she writes, 'The tenth floor of my advent calendar.'

Last year Natalie submitted a poem dedicated to her late university lecturer Nigel Jenkins, entitled 'Jackdaws.' A year on, the memory of Nigel Jenkins remains with us. He encouraged all his students of creative writing at Swansea University to enter the award.

Richard Lewis, winner of the second prize this year, submitted a carefully-crafted poem, entitled 'Work in Progress.' There is a sense of isolation in his words:

> We stood for a moment,
> the trees grow old and bald and bitter.
> The cold lets itself in…

The third winning entry of this year's award is a story entitled 'Rossiya.' Eluned Gramich captures the imagination of the reader. The two characters involved in the story have been friends since childhood. Not only are they very different, they also have different dreams and aspirations. The subject of the story is a shared holiday travelling through Russia by train. The author includes good use of dialogue, as well as conflict and suspense.

It has been very rewarding to receive entries from all parts of Wales. During the summer of 2014, a past winner of the award, poet Glyn Edwards, was reading at the Wordpress Festival in North Wales. He volunteered to promote the award and to sell *Cheval* anthologies. Attending the festival was poet and writer Ellie Jones. Ellie was particularly impressed with the anthology, *Cheval 7*, and is encouraging new young writers in the area to enter the award. Ellie at one time produced a study guide on the poet R.S. Thomas, for use in secondary schools.

The hills of North Wales can be very bleak, and many of the poems of R.S. Thomas describe the harsh conditions of the hill farmer. Similarly, one of the entrants to this year's award has an echo of R.S. Thomas' theme in her story, 'Economical.' The scene is set by the author, Eleanor Butler, in the mountains above the town of Hope in North Wales. This very moving story illustrates the harsh life experienced by a hill farmer's wife who is trapped within the isolation of her surroundings.

It is particularly pleasing to see young writers remain involved in the Terry Hetherington Young Writers' Award, such as Jonathan Edwards, who has edited *Cheval 8* alongside Alan Perry.

Alan Perry is Welsh editor of a collection of Welsh and Mauritian writing, entitled 'When young Dodos meet young Dragons' (L'Atelier d'écriture of Mauritius). Its Mauritian editors are writers Sachita Samboo and Barlen Pyamootoo. The book includes many writers who achieved success through the Terry Hetherington Award, including Robin Ganderton, Joâo Morais, Siôn Tomos Owen and Jemma King.

Some past winners of the Terry Hetherington Award have gone on to receive further prestigious awards, notably Jonathan Edwards and Tyler Keevil. The progress of young writers, their previous winning stories and poetry can be found on the Cheval website, www.chevalwriters.org.uk. It includes details of books published by past winners. The most recently published writers are Mao Oliver-Semenov, with his book, *Sunbathing in Siberia*, and Georgia Carys Williams, with her collection of stories, *Second-hand Rain*.

Malcolm Lloyd provides the Terry Hetherington Young Writers' Award with the most comprehensive website. Everyone involved admires his technological skills. Included on the website are video clips of the supporters of the award who attend Neath 'Poems and Pints' evenings on the first Thursday of every month. They are the backbone of the award, helping to raise funds. In all weather they attend The Cambrian Arms, Melin, to raise funds for the award. The Cheval trustees truly value their contribution.

The judges for the Terry Hetherington Award, once again, were faced with a most difficult task to find a winner for 2015. The entries have all achieved a very high standard. It has been a pleasure reading everyone's entry. It is not a pleasure having to decide on the winners!

Aida Birch

PREFACE

When I was a child – or a younger child than I am now – I had a very clear vision of the future. By the age of five or so I'd calmly weighed up the pros and cons of the obvious career options – miner, butcher, astronaut, sword swallower – but had set my heart on something far greater. I'd seen him on cartoons, the man I wanted to be: grinning, muscle-bound, fearless, he was capable of soaring to heights that no one else could, of leaving a community gaping in awe. He could even wear a crash helmet and still look damn cool. My path was set. I wanted to be a human cannonball.

My parents were unimpressed. I don't think the fact that I couldn't yet form the words properly and kept telling them passionately that I wanted to be a human cannibal helped the situation any. A decade or so later, choosing a subject for university, I went for English. It wasn't being a human cannonball but it was, sort of, cartoons, and I found there something which reminded me of my childhood ambition. In *On the Road*, Sal Paradise describes his friends in these terms:

> They danced down the streets like dingledodies, and
> I shambled after as I've been doing all my life after
> people who interest me, because the only people for

me are the mad ones, the ones who are mad to live, mad to talk, mad to be saved, desirous of everything at the same time, the ones who never yawn or say a commonplace thing, but burn, burn, burn like fabulous yellow roman candles exploding like spiders across the stars and in the middle you see the blue centerlight pop and everybody goes 'Awww!'

Reading the submissions for *Cheval 8* reminded me again of my love of the human cannonball. The image has a particular resonance, perhaps, for the writers whose work is collected in the second section of this anthology, who have won or been commended in the award in previous years. Since being fired out of the cannon of early success with the Terry Hetherington Award, these writers' work has continued to soar, as the readers of Wales – and in many cases the world – have looked up in awe. Tyler Keevil has published two novels and a short story collection, winning the prestigious Journey Prize in Canada and the People's Choice at the Wales Book of the Year. Anna Lewis has published a wonderful collection of poems with Parthian and her follow-up pamphlet is due from Rack Press. As an editor, I also count myself very lucky to be able to include here some short stories by Thomas Morris. His debut collection, *We Don't Know What We're Doing*, will be published by Faber & Faber this August, and I have enough faith in the intelligence and discernment of readers around the country to know that, by the time we come to put together *Cheval 9*, it will have made him famous.

But what of this year's human cannonballs? Turning to the entries for 2015, one way in which *Cheval 8* might be described is as, to appropriate its publisher's marketing, a carnival of voices. Luke Smith's 'No More Bets Please' takes on what has emerged as an important issue for so many living in Wales this past year, giving us the experience of someone addicted to fixed odds gambling machines, in a voice which will be enjoyable for all of us familiar with the work of writers like Irvine Welsh. Jessica Winterton's 'The Oozlum Bird' gives us such a well-drawn narrator, whose character roars from the page from the first time we meet him, speeding up the A65 in his new Land Rover. And in Lowri Llewelyn-Astley's 'Melon,' we meet Dolly, a brilliantly-drawn character or, to put it better, human being. This shocking story is one of the most powerful and memorable pieces of fiction I have read for a very long time.

So there they go then, the writers, queuing up in their crash helmets, those grins they get from knowing something we don't, waiting for their turn in our rickety little cannon. The judges of the Terry Hetherington Award – Aida Birch, Phil Knight, Alan and Jean Perry, Huw Pudner – stand there like the mischievous, mercurial, endlessly supportive and encouraging wonders I know they are. They're fiddling with matches, ready to light the fuse on the careers of these writers, as they have done for so many of us. One of this year's winners climbs boldly into the cannon now and settles themselves in. A pop and a crash and they're off, sailing through the sky, illuminating the world, giving us something to bloody look at. So go on and look up with me then, readers, in awe, in wonder. Let your jaws gape open now. Go 'Awww!'

Jonathan Edwards

ACKNOWLEDGEMENTS

The trustees would like to thank everyone who's supported *Cheval* and the Terry Hetherington Award with their generous donations of time and money. These include Eirwyn Evans, John Lloyd James, Linda and Stan Kinsey and Ellie Jones. Thanks are also due to our loyal Neath 'Poems and Pints' supporters – including both musicians and writers – at our poetry evenings in Briton Ferry; to bar staff Gavin and Bill as well as Colin and Dewi, the ever-hospitable landlords of The Cambrian pub; and also to our three stalwart volunteers, Kym, Brendan and Liza Osborne, whose help at Cheval events has proved invaluable.

The continued involvement and assistance of Richard Lewis Davies, Claire Houguez and Robert Harries of Parthian Books has raised the prestige of the Terry Hetherington Award, and helped further the careers of many of our young writers. Past winners and contributors to *Cheval* have gone on to have first, and even second, books published – or due for publication – as well as winning a host of awards along the way and we congratulate the likes of Jonathan Edwards, Jemma L. King, Anna Lewis, Thomas Morris, Tyler Keevil, Mao Oliver-Semenov, Katherine Stansfield and Georgia Carys Williams, among others, on their successes. Happily, this list is a long and constantly growing one and we are more than happy to be still publishing their generous contributions of recent work in *Cheval*.

Jo Furber of the Dylan Thomas Centre has graciously hosted all our Terry Hetherington Award evenings and we are indebted to her and Alan Kellermann for their ongoing and unstinting support.

The five judges for the Terry Hetherington Award are Aida Birch, Phil Knight, Huw Pudner and Jean and Alan Perry. Thanks are also due to our administrator, Amanda Birch, for making all our jobs a lot easier, and to Malcolm Lloyd, who works so hard to manage and update our website at www.chevalwriters.org.uk.

We thank everyone who submitted work for the award. Some tough decisions had to be made in selecting work for this anthology and many very worthy entries had to be left out for reasons of space.

As usual, all donations and proceeds from raffles, entry fees and the sale of this and other books will go towards financing next year's award.

CHEVAL 8

Terry Hetherington

The Gift

You of the earth, of the colour in a sound,
and the night's eye poised above me,
and I, stumbling through the knowledge
of my need for you,
hearing my rough-hewn tongue
touch on a rare finesse,
to claim this dreaming moment
as my own.
The night absorbs the murmur of a word,
the rhythms shift and change,
and sound becomes the song
held in your giving.

Movement

A dry stone wall crowns the hill.
I lean on it, the cold
rock-lumps against my chest,
and at my back
a frost-bound rippled field.

Before me steeply falls the hill,
then swells out gently, forms a mound,
drops again, shelves and slopes,
twists and bucks, always down
towards the town where slated
roofs run in rows,
on and on, straight and true,
twine and turn, rise and fall,
fly off at tangents,
slew and lean, climb and slide.
Then to my side,
intruding movement – tangible –
a distant fox invades my eye,
one moment's blur, he makes the gorse.
I turn again, see a slope,
see the town:
all movement gone.

Emily Blewitt

How to Explain *Hiraeth* to an Englishman

Take greyhounds. Ignore the words your village vicar slurred about souls from his tired pulpit all those years ago in Wrington; instead consider that greyhounds make excellent pets. They can be friends with other greyhounds, children and cats. Though they can reach speeds of up to 40mph, greyhounds are couch potatoes. Greyhounds are stylish, frequently seen wearing scarves, snoods and leg warmers. Greyhounds are sight hounds and can sometimes lose their way.

To find a greyhound, you can follow the smell of chips into Cardiff town centre, or google Greyhound Rescue Centre Wales. Names for greyhounds include Ballymac Kay, Coppice Socks, Stanley, Pat, Witch's Bravo, Tip-ex and Noodles. My favourite greyhound is Noodles – the advert says you can just add hot water and chaos ensues and shows him nose to nose with three pampered cats on a bed. Apparently he needs a bit of training to become 'a more balanced diet'.

Once, I was leant on by a greyhound dozing standing up, and when he opened his eyes I swear they said *Hiraeth.*

So when you puzzle through these streets, feeling lost to this west country that is no West Country, look into the eyes of that animal, the one whose coat is mottled fawn, brindle-flanked so you can count each rib, whose longing burns in muscled limbs and who quietly sits, politely waiting, knowing beneath his homeless layers that greyhounds cannot live outdoors, that greyhounds make excellent pets.

Hiraeth is one of those untranslatable Welsh words that roughly means 'the soul's longing for home.'

Pisces Rising

My American friend is pregnant. She swims
lengths on her back, her domed belly

nosing the air like a friendly shark.
When we pause at the side, she asks

How is your boo? – your sweetheart?
– meaning you, and I say

Oh he's fine, he just doesn't like
swimming; for a water sign

he doesn't like getting his feet wet,
hates drying them afterwards.

She laughs and says *Mine grew up*
in a cabin in the woods, with a hippy mother;

he didn't have hot water 'til he was ten.
He must be earth, I say,

mine's from the West Country; he has a
hippy mother too. Then, shyly: I'm air

but when we go flying, flying
to New York, no less – I can't bear

to look out the window, though we've filed past
first class to my people in economy, the honeymooners

making eyes next to us, and we're skipping, skimming
the tarmac, full-in-flight when the lights come on and I
realise oh god

I'm bleeding, I'm bleeding so heavy I have to keep unbuckling
and wending my way to the bathroom, I've abandoned

my knitting and the only thing that keeps me kneading
my thighs and back to ease the cramps

is his leaning whisper:
Guess what? I love you,

and he catches my tears through
my smile in the palm of his hand.

The Philobrutist

Give me the man who keeps a lead in the boot of his car for
rescuing loose dogs.
I want him crouching, shooing daft pairs of ducks out of
oncoming traffic;
I want the pavement lined with dandelions he steps deftly
over, open-palmed.

I want his humane mousetraps, the miniature fences he
makes from Cadbury's fingers
to send him out jogging at 3am, so two fat rodents can taste
chocolate and freedom
in a wildflower meadow. I want him to fix a broken radio

and rig up three extension cables from the garage, so a
budgerigar can sing and bob
and see out of a window. I want his unerring, unnerving
birdsong whistle;
I want him to bathe his mum's tortoise every morning

and dry her carefully on old newspaper, while explaining
how her shell's nerve-endings
respond unexpectedly to touch. I want him when he matter-
of-factly

puts peanut butter sandwiches out for the badgers. I want him
to lay his hands

on my shoulders and loosen the knot at the nape of my neck
and I want
to stand on his feet while he spins me in circles. I want him so
badly I'm giddy
and ravenous; I want him to follow me, follow me home.

Aimee Bray
(Highly Commended)

Persephone's Underworld

My mother planted bulbs in the autumn. Deep, deep down into the earth, where it's still warm, where things die and then grow again. I knew I'd be returning to the Underground soon – the record store, that is – and, like clockwork, a blanket of winter depression smothered me.

For 3 years I had a job that spanned from November to the end of January, picking through old discs, pushing the top albums on an array of customers. A cash-in-hand kind of job. It was dank, in the basement of a book shop, literally *underground*.

It might have been less depressing if I didn't live with my grandparents for the duration. Midway between my college and work, I drifted between the two all winter. Mam and I talked every few days, but it was a strange feeling. Warm plastic pressed against my ear and a fissure in my chest. Her voice sounding so far away.

'Fancy something? I got crisps, flapjacks. Anything.'

Hayden, my boss. He offered me food all the time, but I never once said yes. Sometimes, after an eight hour shift, my stomach was howling. I suppose I looked for the hidden things, for the reasons to say no. When people give you something, it feels like an act of claiming. He was good looking, in an older sort of way: dark eyes; the shadow of a beard; pale, skeletal fingers. Mid-thirties, at least.

'You should accept my offerings. I don't give my food to just anyone.' He wagged a finger at me, laughing. He had this little sinister persona when he showed off. I smiled back, sometimes, but regretted it.

*

I was there for the winter of his divorce.

'Ah kid, don't ever get married. You're too sweet for that. It'll ruin you.' I remember him being particularly unshaven that day. He looked like hell.

'£2.01 change,' I muttered, blushing, as I thrust the coins into the woman's hand. She kept glancing at Hayden, but he ignored her.

'*Women*. You'll do anything for them. God, I jumped through hoops for her. Nothing was ever good enough though. And now look at me. *Old*.'

'You're not that old.'

It was a knee-jerk reaction, perched on the tongue, ready. I swallowed, regretting the words.

He smiled, ducking his head as if I'd pleased him. I shivered; it was always cold here, deep down in the basement. We were both lonely, I think, except I cloaked myself in it.

*

When I told my mam about Hayden's divorce, she sighed.

'Nothing ever lasts does it?'

She always made questions sound like statements.

'Some things do. Maybe.'

'You're right. Things end. New things start. The circle of life.' She laughed; her eyes glowed.

Next winter, while closing up, Hayden helped me haul a stack of albums into the storage room. He fumbled with the switch, swearing – 'Fuck it' – but it remained dark. We deposited the albums on the floor, but he still didn't move. The faint light seemed to cling to my hair, glittering, and enhancing the shadows of his face. The space shrunk around us. He had this strange look in his eyes, an ancient stare. I felt like I could taste the air, it was so charged.

'Did I forget something?' I bit my lip.

He looked a little dumbfounded for a moment, shaking his head. 'Only your sense.' He cleared his throat, laughed, and we left the room before I could say anything else.

*

Summer never ends, until it does. It feels perpetual. The warmer months, just me and my mam, my college work and friends. I was a different person. Mam had this way of making things grow around her.

A late summer evening with mam, helping her water her garden. Her hair glinted white-gold in the sun, curled like a Greek goddess. She probably couldn't even feel the approaching winter. I did.

'Beth sy'n bod?'

Her latest big idea was to learn another language. She didn't know more than a few words yet, though knowing her she'd be fluent come spring.

'Nothing.'

'Silly.' She tucked her arm around my head, kissed my forehead. She smelt of earth.

'I hate the cold,' I found myself saying.

'It's not that bad. It's only September.'

'It will be soon.'

I pushed the geranium seeds into the pot, spreading compost with my fingers. Come February they'd explode in purple.

'You're good at that.'

I said nothing.

'What's wrong?'

I didn't know. It was a growing apprehension, dark on the horizon.

'All the plants will die soon.'

'Well that's a cheerful way of looking at things!'

'How else is there?'

'Oh, baban.' She sighed. 'They'll be sleeping. They'll be back again in spring.'

I rolled my eyes. Mam, the idealist.

*

Looking back, I suppose it's all very obvious. At the time, I buried myself in the menial tasks. Internally counting out my savings; arranging the CD spines alphabetically; controlling the playlist (Hayden always said that it was all about the *atmosphere*). The store could get pretty busy, particularly before Christmas. Sometimes we went the whole day without speaking. Me, sitting at the register with my history coursework; him, rummaging in the back room, humming.

At the end of January, I got this strange hopeful bubble in my stomach. It meant that the end was approaching. It felt like being thawed out. Next winter would be my last ever winter before I left for uni, for good. I smiled to myself, shivering under my thick cardigan. I hit forward on the remote for the CD player.

Hayden popped his head out from behind an aisle at the burst of a familiar guitar solo.

'Christ. These guys again?' He liked to poke fun at my music.

'Hey! They're good.'

He pulled a face, mock disappointment. I laughed, and then he just stopped smiling. He walked up to the counter, looming over the centre of my vision. There were no windows, so the lighting was always artificially bright. It made the lines on his face seem deeper, darker.

'Last day tomorrow,' I murmured. My mouth felt dry; it sounded like a croak.

'Yeah.'

I don't know how it happened. For a moment, I didn't even react. He leant down and kissed me. I was frozen in surprise; my arms hung at my side. His lips were crushing. I jerked away, shoving him in the chest.

'What?' My mouth just hung open, stupidly.

He blinked.

'What did you just do?' My throat felt tight. Why did I want to cry? My hands fluttered to my face.

'Oh no. Oh God. Sephy, I'm so sorry. I thought –'

'You can't *do* that!' I tried to shout; I sounded strangled. 'You're *old*. I mean, you're not –'

'Ok.' His eyes were stricken. He touched my shoulder. 'I'm so sorry, I've just been lonel–'

'Stop! You can't do that! You can't do that!'

'Please, stay. *Please*.'

His presence was like a weight in the air, in my lungs. Affecting everything. But I needed the Underground: for the money, for uni, for … him? I had to get out of there. I couldn't breathe. I stood up, blocking out his words, and ran away. Outside, it was dark, just like when I'd arrived in the morning. Nothing had changed.

*

'Mam?'

'Hey, love.' A yawn. 'It's late.'

'Yeah, sorry.'

'Are you ok?'

The phone shook in my hands.

'It's only for one more day,' she said.

'I hate it here. I miss you.'

'I miss you, too. I hate it when you're away.'

'Then why do you let me leave?'

'I thought it's what you wanted.' She laughed a little. 'All the plants die when you're away.'

'Don't be silly; you're the gardener.'

She laughed again. 'Not like you. Chin up, my little Persephone.'

*

The following morning, I felt like I was armouring myself up for war. I had to stand up to him, tell him I was leaving forever. I meant to say so many things.

'Hey, Sephy.'

He looked so sad.

'Hey.'

It was my last day. There weren't many customers. We both went through the motions, while our own internal storms raged. I pretended not to notice when he looked at me. His quiet presence was like gravity, a sun absorbing all the helpless little planets. At closing time, I got up to leave. I needed to tear myself away from this hole before it swallowed me up for good.

'Wait, Sephy. I'm sorry.'

I nodded. This was it. I was going to let everything out, explode. I'm leaving. I'm not coming back. I'll never be back. All I could think was how sad he looked. A coldness expanded

14

in my chest as he looked at me. Like a flower shrivelling in the cold, I faltered and said, 'See you next winter.'

He half-smiled, relieved, and dropped his head.

Eleanor Butler

Economical

The bank of clouds rolling in from behind the mountain was a familiar sight; the darkness of the steel grey mass stretched across a leaden sky, as flinty as the land below, and as unyielding as the people who farmed it. She looked up from the yard, leaning on the rake, and shielded her eyes from the strong sun beams which valiantly fought the inevitable rain. As the first spots splattered her face and overcoat, she spun wildly, searching for the glimmer of a rainbow, desperately seeking the splash of colour amidst the drabness of her surroundings. It stretched up and over the farmhouse, across the fields and the large, purple mass of Mynydd yr Hob, and down into the village behind it. Isolated on the mountain farm in her high solitude, with no one but Ted and the dogs to talk to, was it any wonder the rainbow taunted her with suggestions of the gold at the other end? Bitterly, she spat on the floor and resumed her task of cleaning before the rain came in earnest to ruin her hard work. If she had known the meaning of irony she would have laughed, for the rainbow's arch was uncannily accurate, pointing down into the village named Hope and to the companionship she craved, down to the golden glow of golden lights they could see on clear nights on top of the peak. From inside the house, the grandfather clock could be heard booming the hour to the silent hall, and she hurried to the cowshed with her tools, anxious not to be late for Ted again. Covering her hair with the heavy overcoat, she made the final dash back across the year, seeking shelter within the porch to watch the last shimmer of the rainbow let go as the rain fell, washing clean the wishes that lay within its graceful arch.

The clock struck again, and again she peered out of the kitchen window to where the track curved down from the mountain to the house. She had repeated this ritual for three hours and still there was no sign of Ted and the dogs, her only company the steady tick of the clock counting the seconds, minutes and hours away. She fingered the loose threads on her apron and worried her lip. If she called the village and it was nothing – if she was just over reacting – was it worth the storm of fury? She dallied for a few more moments, craning her neck around to catch a glimpse of a felt hat and a flick of a tail, but again the track was empty. Resolved, she crossed the room to where the telephone lay in its cradle and hurriedly made the connection to the police. As she waited to be put through, a bark filtered into the kitchen and a wave of something, not quite relief, washed over her. She placed the telephone back down into the cradle before Ted could see her and guess her intentions. Standing by the heavy stone sink, she saw him make his way cautiously down the muddy track with something cradled in his arms. Heart in her mouth, she wondered if she should prepare the bed for what could only be a lamb, probably motherless and ill. Her eyes flicked to the corner of the fire, already making a mental list of the paraphernalia she would need to care for it, dreading the long nights and the extra work load. She paused for him to enter the house with his bundle but again she was left waiting. Exasperated and irritated, she pulled on her outside boots and stomped across the yard, riled at the thought of the hours wasted looking out of the window in expectation. If it had been the other way round, if *he* had had to wait for *her*…it didn't bear thinking about. She followed the noise of barking, sure that Ted would have his usual entourage of adoring dogs around him. The noise exuded from the barn and yet, as she turned the corner, she stumbled into her husband as he came out of the shed, his arms full of rope.

'Aye', he grunted to her, making his way towards the source of noise. Her curiosity aroused, she followed him towards the stone building. Abruptly, he stopped in the doorway and turned to her.

'No girl. Get away now, you hear?'

He shook his head and gestured back to the house with a dismissive flick of his stick. Forever economical with his words. Forever adding to her loneliness. Daring for once, perhaps fuelled by the overwhelming sense of injustice she battled daily to keep from bursting through her usual restraint, she pushed past the old man with impatience and entered the barn. Confused, she looked for the lamb, but her eyes only landed on one of the dogs, whimpering and whining from the corner. In the gloom of the barn it was hard to make out, but as she got closer she saw the angle at which he was holding his leg. Sadness filled her eyes as she understood what Ted had come here to do. She looked around for his gun but saw only the rope he had brought, coiled snakelike in his arms.

'The gun, Ted, where is it?'

He shook his head and picked up the rope, swinging it over one of the beams. She knew better to repeat herself and waited, her heart in her mouth, her eyes transfixed by the swaying end of fibres above.

'Go on girl.' He tossed his head towards the house and she knew better than to argue with the hardness of his tone this time. With one last stroke of the dog's head she left, head down, anxious to be back in the safety of the kitchen. As she turned the corner towards the house the whimpers crescendo-ed in a discordant symphony to terrible heights, cut short at the climax by an invisible conductor. Silence lay like a suffocating blanket over the farm buildings and the overbearing presence of the mountain seemed even more oppressive than usual. A whimper of her own escaped her mouth and she increased her pace. Through the sleeting rain, the blurry outline of a gun could be seen propped up just inside the porch door.

Later, at dinner, serenaded only by the constant ticking of the clock from the hall, she asked why, breaking the habitual silence lying between them. Ted stopped, too surprised at the interruption to be disgruntled and almost shrugged off the question. She waited, expecting the inevitable dismissal from the room.

'And waste a good bullet on a dog?'

He snorted in scorn and resumed his methodical eating. Stunned, she sat across from the man. Economical to the end.

Jenni Derrick

On the Pier

Bare chest boys cast
their lines, with spindly arms,
and furtive glances down the pier
at the shirtless men.

Puffing out their chests,
they try to cast bigger shadows,
as they wait for the tug on the line
that will give them a story to tell.

'It nearly broke my rod.'
'Almost pulled me in.'
'I got it though.'

These words the beer-inflated men remember well.

Unaware they're idols, the men glance up the pier,
remembering how it was to stand there
at the edge.

What they wouldn't give to be there again.

With sticky-out collar bones
and skin that fitted their frames.
To hold that first catch.
The one that would always keep growing.

The Happy Man

for Cameron

They didn't even realise they were sad.
Lost in that tunnel for so long,
they had forgotten there was light outside.

But you had always been able to
see through it.

You believed you could guide them out.
Perhaps by shouting loud enough
they would be able to follow your voice,
and see that tunnels always end.

But they never came.
Like beetles preferring to remain in the gloom,
because in the damp darkness they are kings.

I thought you were going to
crawl into the tunnel after them.
Instead you sighed and asked:
'Why don't they want to be happy?'

And then you, the Happy Man, cried for all the sadness
in the world.
And because you could not halt everybody's tears.

Tom Gatehouse

The Other Tower

Martinelli sat in the empty apartment waiting for the furniture to arrive. He still did not have a chair, so he sat on the floor, a pack of cigarettes, an ashtray and a lighter by his side. At intervals he would get up, and pace around barefoot, running his hands over the walls, along the windowsills. It was a small place, but it suited his needs, a top-floor apartment in a neighbourhood a little removed from the fashionable districts in the south of the city, but quieter, and far more affordable. There were a couple of good bars nearby, a buffet for lunch on the days he worked from home, and it was close to one of the city's best parks.

The furniture came later that evening. Two surly delivery-men hauled it up all five flights of stairs. Dumping it in the hallway, one of them presented Martinelli with a copy of the invoice to sign. As soon as he handed it back to them, they marched out of the apartment and back down the stairs. He did not even have a chance to offer them a glass of water.

Sabrina came over the next day. Squeezing past the boxes in the hallway, she stood in the middle of his empty living room, hands on hips, looking around the place.

'Well?'

'It has potential. Can I smoke?'

He nodded, sliding the ashtray towards her with his foot.

She went over to the window and pulled it all the way open.

'And you even have a sea view, sort of,' she said, leaning out.

'Really? I hadn't noticed.'

'Come here.' She shuffled along the windowsill so that he could lean out with her. 'Look. Over there. That blue stripe in between those towers in the distance.'

'Isn't that just the sky?'

'Don't be daft, it's a different colour. It's a darker blue.'

'You're right,' he said.

'You're lucky. They normally charge more for that.'

'Maybe they already have.'

The two of them stayed there for a minute, looking out over the city. Green hills swelled up out of the sprawl, shantytowns speckling their flanks. Further downtown, the office blocks, hotels and high rises, glittering in the light, and beyond them, that blue brushstroke on the horizon.

'Shall we get to work?' asked Sabrina. 'I assume you'll want a hand with all of this.'

They worked all day, slicing the boxes open with kitchen knives, removing all the plastic and polystyrene inside, then easing out his furniture and appliances. He flooded his kitchen while installing the washing machine, which set them back an hour or two while they waited for the floor to dry. They narrowly avoided a furious argument during the assembly of his kitchen table, finally concluding that it was defective, as it wobbled every time any weight was placed on it. Martinelli was forced to jam a piece of cardboard under one of its legs. Even his divan was awkward to set up. He was reduced to hacking at the fabric underneath it so he could screw the feet in. At the end of the day, the two of them sat slumped on his futon (the one thing that had been easy to set up), smoking in silence, the ashtray between them.

He resolved to try and do at least one thing for the apartment every day: buy some more utensils for his kitchen, put some posters on the walls, unpack his books and put them on the shelves. He found homes for his plants. He put his magnetic words on his fridge, his fortune cat on top. He unpacked his suitcase and hung his shirts, jackets and trousers in the wardrobe. The wall by his bed sprouted photos: his family, some old friends, one or two holiday pictures.

He had been in the apartment for more than a week when the noises started.

It happened on a Friday morning, at about half past seven. There was a sequence of two or three thick, guttural sounds, each lasting just a second or less. Not unlike the bark of a large dog, though afterwards Martinelli thought they sounded like some kind of primate, a howler monkey, or a gorilla perhaps. They were followed by a banging, so hard and fast it made his walls and furniture shake. It lasted for a few seconds and then stopped.

He sat up in bed, wide-awake, the blood throbbing in his temples. His first thought was that there was someone at the door. He got out of bed and tiptoed out of his bedroom and down the hallway. He put his eye to the spy-hole. There was nobody there: just the landing, empty except for his bicycle and an old pot of paint the decorators had left in one corner. He padded his way into the kitchen and put the kettle on. He was waiting for the coffee to brew when the banging started again, but this time, it was followed by a loud scream. He stood in his kitchen in his underwear, transfixed by the sound. Scream wasn't exactly the right word. It was more of a roar. It could have been coming from a wild animal, were it not for the torrent of expletives he managed to distinguish amid the sound. It stopped abruptly after a few seconds. Then there was silence.

A couple of weeks passed. Sabrina came round one day after work with a new plant, which he put on top of his bookshelves. She helped him hang pictures, move furniture.

He had a modest housewarming one Friday night, ten or fifteen people squeezed into his small living room, talking loud over his record player, the windows open to the night. He still listened out for the banging, but had begun to dismiss it as a bizarre one-off. Then it happened a second time.

It was a little earlier than before, around seven o'clock. The same sequence of sounds: the odd monkey noises, followed by a fierce banging, so intense it made the walls shake, accompanied by someone roaring like a large animal in pain. Waking from a deep sleep, Martinelli didn't realise at first what was happening. It took him a second to remember. He sat up in bed listening to the sound, his heart beating fast. It was so loud it was as if it were coming from inside his own apartment, or perhaps from next door. But there was no next door as such. The building was divided into two towers with a shared lobby on the ground floor. There were two apartments on every floor except the top, where there was just a single apartment on each side.

One morning Martinelli was coming down the stairs with his bicycle when he ran straight into the caretaker in the lobby. The old man was polishing one of the big mirrors that ran the length of one wall.

'Careful young man, you nearly had my head off with that thing.'

'Sorry,' said Martinelli.

'Mind you don't wheel it along the floor as well, I've just mopped.'

'Of course. Listen, I wanted to ask you about something...'

'Yes?'

'You live in the other tower, right?'

'I do.'

'You haven't been hearing any banging, have you? In the mornings.'

'Banging? What, like, building work?'

'No,' said Martinelli. 'It sounds like someone hammering on the walls with their hands. It's woken me up a couple of times now. And it's always followed by them shouting at the top of their voice.'

The caretaker scratched the side of his nose with a finger. 'No, I can't say I've heard anything like that. But then I'm getting a bit hard of hearing these days. Which floor did you say you lived on?'

'The top floor of this block.'

'That'll be why then. I don't think the noise would carry down to my apartment.'

'Maybe not. But that's the strange thing: if the noise is coming from my level, then it's coming from the other tower. I wouldn't have thought it would carry that far either.'

'I don't know,' said the caretaker. 'Perhaps if they kept their window open it would. Let me know if it happens again, and if anyone else mentions it I'll make some inquiries.'

'Thanks,' said Martinelli.

One evening he was dismounting from his bicycle outside the main entrance of the building, when the caretaker came over.

'How are the noises?' he said. 'Any more since the last time we spoke?'

'Not since the last time, no.'

'Come and meet the people who live on the top floor of the other tower. You can ask them if they've heard anything.'

Martinelli hoisted his bicycle up onto his shoulder and followed the old man into the lobby. At the foot of the staircase leading up into the other tower there stood a woman and a young man of about Martinelli's age. The woman was in late middle age, her round face framed by a cloud of bushy brown hair. He offered her his hand.

'Luiz. Nice to meet you.'

She gave a limp handshake in return. 'Sandra. And this is my son, William.'

Martinelli offered his hand to William, who just looked blankly down at it. Then he looked at Martinelli for a moment, before diverting his eyes and shying away. Martinelli let his hand drop, eyeing the young man with interest. He was chewing hard on his bottom lip, while his gaze moved all over the lobby, jumping from object to object.

'Don't mind him,' said Sandra. 'He can be a little shy with people he doesn't know. The caretaker said you wanted to ask us about something?'

'Uh...' Martinelli began. He looked again at William, who was making these strange movements with his mouth, as if trying to dislodge a piece of food from behind his molars with his tongue. Martinelli looked back to Sandra. 'You, uh... you haven't heard any banging in the mornings, have you?'

'What kind of banging?'

'I've heard it a couple of times since I moved in. Like someone banging on the walls with the palms of their hands and their fists. And they scream as well. Always around seven, half seven in the morning. I find it rather unsettling.'

'Well I'm not surprised! That sounds awful. But no, we've not heard anything. I'm always up at that time, so I'd be sure to hear it.'

He stared at her. 'You're quite sure of that?'

'Positive. Perhaps it's coming from an apartment in the building next door. It's funny the way sound carries round these apartment blocks.'

He thanked her and they parted. As he tramped up the stairs it occurred to him that he might have been dreaming the noises, but he quickly dismissed the idea. He had never dreamt with that level of detail before: his wardrobe door rattling in its runner, the water trembling in a glass on his bedside table.

The following morning it happened again, earlier still this

time. He got out of bed and stalked over to his bedroom window. He slid it open. It was a clear morning, nothing out of the ordinary. The sun had risen. In the apartment block opposite most of the windows still had their blinds down. He craned his head out further, trying to get a view into the apartment in the other tower, about fifteen metres over to his left, but there was no way he could stretch out far enough. He ducked back into his room and was about to pull the window shut when the banging started again. This time there was a flurry of curtain at one of the windows in the building opposite, one floor below his own. The curtains opened and he saw a couple: a bare-chested young man, about his own age, glaring up at the window parallel to his own, and a girl in a long T-shirt, leaning on her boyfriend's shoulder. Martinelli managed to catch the girl's eye. She pointed in the direction of the noise and mouthed something to him. Then the young man saw him, gave him a curt nod, and pulled the curtains shut. Martinelli closed the window and sat on the edge of the bed, thinking.

When the banging started again on Wednesday the following week, he got out of bed without a clear idea of what exactly he was going to do. He slipped on some clothes, and ran down the stairs and into the lobby. The noises became duller and more distant with every floor that he descended, replaced by the noise of his flip-flops slapping on the hard floors and echoing up the empty staircase. He ran through the deserted lobby, entered the other tower, and began ascending. After a floor or two, he began to hear the noises again, the volume becoming louder the closer he got to the top. On the last flight of stairs, the noises stopped. In the silence, he stopped his dash up the stairs, and walked the last few steps, catching his breath. The landing was identical to his own, minus the bicycle and the pot of paint. His breathing heavy, he went over to the door and knocked, three times. He heard voices inside stop and footsteps come over to the door. Sandra opened it.

'Oh…' she began, but before she could go on Martinelli had already barged past her into the apartment.

'I just want to have a word with your son,' he said.

The woman just stuttered, at a loss for words.

Martinelli ducked into the two bedrooms, but he couldn't see the young man anywhere. Finally, he looked into the kitchen. There he was, sitting at a table laid out for breakfast. There was a flask of coffee on the table, a breadbasket, a sandwich toaster. William was eating a bowl of cereal. He didn't seem surprised to see Martinelli at all, and gave him a big toothy grin. Before Martinelli could say anything, William opened his mouth wide to show him the food he had been chewing, a grey-brown mess that fell off his tongue and into his lap. Martinelli just stared at him. As the milk dribbled down his chin, William laughed, spraying the tablecloth with white droplets. Sandra, tugging at Martinelli's sleeve, was finally able to lead him out of the kitchen, down the passage, and out of the apartment.

'Don't think I won't tell the caretaker about this,' she was saying. 'In all the years I've lived here, I've never known anything like it…'

'I'm sorry…' Martinelli said.

The door closed in his face. He sat down on the top step. In the apartment behind him, he could hear Sandra clattering the breakfast things. There was a sudden shriek of laughter. Then silence.

Windmills of Groningen

The dust motes flicker in the light of mornings
that daily evade the shutter's capture.
Waves seethe beneath a door closed
to the petitions of unruly suitors,
their calls falling on ears deaf
to the everyday.
                  Her yawns ripple
indifferent through long afternoons,
her lashes falling heavy and ironic
upon peace offerings wrapped
in brown paper. You hide contrite
eyes behind leaves.
                  For the flutter
in her arteries is a code you have
always misread. In the crosshairs,
your stale breath twists the vine,
the snow falling hard now upon
the terracotta.
                  But this is just
the rumble of distant thunder. You
would not dare shoot your mouth,
risk the wing of a cabbage white.
Her feet remain, fragile as ever,
pale, like the sunlight.

Concerning an Unlikely
Femme Fatale

'Embarrassing,' you said. Yes, I admit it.
She did rather get the best of me.
But little did you know your turn would come,
And how! The two of you failed miserably
To keep the lid on your springtime kisses,
Which, by autumn, had gone rank like bad milk.
Oh yes, that treacherous undertow
Sucked you so far out we lost hope of ever
Hauling you back. You washed up later
Just like the rest of us, breathless, penitent.
She left a trail of maxed-out overdrafts,
Broken drums, atrocious poems and songs.
Witchcraft? Even worse. She was the damsel
We were fool enough to think we could save.

Urban Villanelle

The drunk rocks out in the street on Tuesday night.
Won't some Samaritan please take him home?
All those present agree, what an unpleasant sight.

The buskers just play, ignoring him outright.
His chops are grizzled, his gut overgrown.
The drunk rocks out in the street on Tuesday night.

The guitar is layered; the bass and drums are tight.
The drunk gurns and pouts, as if he were alone.
All those present agree, what an unpleasant sight.

The drunk plods and staggers, but remains upright.
With eyes glazed, he plays air guitar in the zone,
As he rocks out in the street on Tuesday night.

Some avert their gaze, trying to be polite,
While others film him openly on their phones.
All those present agree, what an unpleasant sight.

A little boy points and laughs, in spite
Of Daddy tutting and hurrying him home.
All those present agree, what an unpleasant sight.
The drunk rocks out in the street on Tuesday night.

Eluned Gramich
(Third Prize)

Rossiya

Russia's number one train, the Rossiya, pulled into the Siberian village of Erofei Pavlovich. The pale yellow rectangles of the carriage windows were the only source of light in the midnight dark. There was no sign of the village of Erofei Pavlovich. The walls of the station house blurred into the black sky so that it seemed never-ending. Above its double-door, the word 'Exit' was illuminated by the train's headlights. Beyond the tracks, the world stopped.

The Rossiya's Russian passengers filed out onto the platform. Kathryn burst out like a cat shooting through the back door. Erin followed shuffling, her head heavy with sleep. Unlike the Russians, who wore dressing gowns and old tracksuits, the two English travellers chose tight jeans and lycra vests. The waitress and the cook had their black and white uniforms; the conductor, naturally, wore his official badges and peaked cap. The Rossiya let out a plume of smoke, a long sigh of relief after the journey.

Erin wrapped her scarf around her neck. She didn't want to be outside in the cold: all that was Kathryn's fault. She'd insisted. Erin watched with barely concealed disapproval as Kathryn started on her stretches: forward bends, lunges, reaching her thin arms towards the clouds. It's the middle of the night, for Christ's sake, she thought.

'It's so nice to be out in the fresh air!' Kathryn exclaimed, her breath visible in the cold.

'It stinks of smoke,' Erin said. 'And it's fucking freezing.'

The cook – a large woman who'd been in and out of their cabin all day, trying to sell the last remaining roast chicken – lit a cigarette. Then she lit one for the waitress, who took it without a word and squatted on the platform. The tips of their cigarettes hung like fireflies in the dark. No one spoke. After the noise of the train, the silence was unsettling.

Kathryn started skipping, her breath coming faster.

'Where do you think we are?' she gasped.

'How should I know?'

Erin was nervous. Every night on the train so far, she'd dreamed of being left behind on the platform. These dreams were brutally vivid: the carriage door locked behind her, the freezing wind, her screaming for the train to stop. Sometimes her mother would appear at the window, waving goodbye, ignoring her daughter's desperate cries.

A whistle blew. Erin started. 'That's enough. I'm getting back on,' she said.

'But it's not time to go back yet.'

'Did you check the timetable?'

'Yes.'

'But you always get it wrong.'

'Not true.'

'Remember,' Erin sighed. 'It's Moscow time. It won't be the same as what we think it is.'

'I checked. It's a long stop this time. Fifteen minutes at least.' Kathryn gestured towards the station house. 'Let's go have a look.'

'No,' said Erin. 'Don't be ridiculous.'

'Come on.'

'The train will go without us.'

Kathryn took a step back, teasing, her smile half-concealed by the dark. Another step and Erin wouldn't be able to make out the colour of her clothes. Kathryn pressed, 'Come on, come on.' She was a tall girl: it gave her an advantage, Erin thought, towering over people, overseeing everything. People who were blessed with stature could direct activities and run away from them, as they liked. Of course, it helped that Kathryn was beautiful—a fact strangers acknowledged in the street. Like a model, they told her. Kathryn complained she was 'gangly', and moaned about being flat-chested. To Erin, who barely reached five foot and whose skin hadn't improved since the age of thirteen, any complaint Kathryn made about her appearance was an act of insulting false modesty.

'We'll be stranded,' Erin warned. 'I heard it can happen... A guy at the hostel in Moscow told me. People sprinting after the train when it's already moving. Their passports still in the compartment.'

'Yeah, right.'

'It won't wait for anyone.'

'So what? They survived, didn't they?'

'I don't know. I didn't ask what happened to them.'

Kathryn rolled her eyes up at the sky, muttering under her breath.

'What?' Erin demanded.

'Don't be a coward,' she quickly replied.

'I'm not a coward,' Erin insisted. She glanced longingly at the train, wishing she could be inside; imagining an onward journey of studied solitude: silence and calm. She was anxious for Kathryn to leave. The train manager stood watching them with his fingers curled around a pocket watch. Erin gestured at it. The conductor peered at the clock's round face before solemnly spreading his fingers to indicate the time they had left.

'Just ten minutes,' she translated. The conductor nodded.

'Ten minutes!' Kathryn turned on her heels. 'I bet there's

a shop. We can get beers.'

'You go.'

'Come with me.'

'No, go without me.'

They hadn't bought anything to drink or eat for the last three days. They had the polystyrene packaged meal at twelve o'clock Moscow time from the train kitchen, which they could barely eat. After that, there was hot water from the samovar, served pure. The promise of beer tempted Erin, but still she couldn't bear to be separated from the train. Neither, at this moment, could she bear to be around Kathryn: her constant needling voice pricked Erin's nerves.

'All my things are on the train,' she said.

'So are mine.'

There was a sudden crash as a young family further down the platform closed a carriage door with force. Their baby began to cry; a whine quickly transforming into full-blown sobs. Erin winced. What was ten minutes here, in this complete darkness? she thought. They might forget how long they were away for, misjudge the distance, lose their way. There was no knowing what was waiting there across the tracks.

'For God's sake, Erin.'

The baby reached a crescendo of desperate screams, sending a shoot of pain through Erin's head. 'Just go, will you?' she snapped. 'Go on. Piss off.'

Kathryn shrugged, turned and ran off, swiftly pulling herself up onto the opposite platform, her body unfurling in the direction of the ticket counter like the stem of some long flower.

A moment later and she was gone.

The waitress coughed loudly. The noise made Erin jump. 'Sorry,' she muttered. The waitress squinted at her.

*

They'd known each other from childhood. The primary school where they were desk-sharers, pencil-stealers, hop-scotchers, and the masters of elaborate games. When one yawned, the other followed. When one of them was sick, the other caught it. Even when they grew up, attending the same secondary school, they continued to lie in each other's beds, and tip-toe around each other's family homes like tolerated stray-cats. In the darkness of the long sleepover that made up their childhood, they whispered secrets to each other, close and quiet and honest. Erin would carry those secrets through to adulthood; words she could never forget, because they were so sincere and innocent, so different from anything she said now. One night, Kathryn told Erin she knew she was going to die. And there was nothing she could do to stop it. She was in her sleeping bag, her breath warm against Erin's cheek. The whites of her eyes visible in the dark. Kathryn asked, 'What happens after we die?' Erin knew there was nothing after death because her mother had said so. Erin was too young to understand; the fear of death hadn't reached her yet. So she answered casually, callously, in a way she came to regret: 'We just die. That's it.' Kathryn fell silent. Only a long time afterwards did Erin realise that she too would not be excluded from death.

There's no way of escaping, Erin thought, no way of escaping their childhood selves. They knew too much: bound to each other by a long-acquired knowledge. If Kathryn, an artist, spoke about her work to a group of journalists, Erin immediately thought of her as a teenager: her tantrums – kicking the desk, tearing up exam papers that didn't go well. If Erin, a doctor, offered medical advice to friends, Kathryn recalled the time Erin ate too many chocolates and threw up on her mother's Bohemian silk cushions. Within the net of their friendship, growing up just wasn't possible.

Erin was ambitious – she wanted to be forceful, precise,

competent. Now that her mother was dead, this necessity for self-improvement became more urgent. After the funeral, the first thing she decided to do was go on holiday. To escape. Her mother would have told her to go to the beach, but Erin didn't want to go anywhere which may have reminded her of her mother. She wanted to be alone; prove she didn't need anyone. She wanted to run away from the old, childish Erin.

Kathryn didn't agree with these plans. She explained, 'I need to travel too. Broaden my horizons.' It was raining that day, Erin remembered. The weather had been so awful and she'd been grateful for the tickets to Moscow filed away in her bedside cabinet. Standing in the little kitchen, Kathryn poured a coffee for herself, stirring the sugar with her finger. She grew thoughtful, as if Erin had asked her along on the trip and was now waiting for her answer.

'When are you leaving?' Kathryn wanted to know.

That was when Erin made the mistake of telling her.

*

The conductor raised his right hand, like a Roman emperor hailing an audience. Five minutes.

Erin began to pace. A habit which failed to calm her nerves. Instead it triggered memories of the times she'd set to pacing in the past. Pacing in airports to assuage her fear of flying. In the hospital corridors when her mother was sick. Kathryn, on the other hand, didn't pace. In moments of stress, she simply vanished. Another quality Erin coveted apart from her beauty: this talent for abandonment.

When Erin drove two hours every night to the hospital, with towels and underwear hastily shoved in a plastic bag, it was a young nurse – tall like Kathryn, although less striking – who came and helped Erin change her mother's clothes. When Erin sat in the car on the way back, and cried in floods of self-pity because she knew she'd be an orphan at twenty-six, it was the radio presenter who comforted her with a joke. When Erin helped her mother to the commode four times a night, it was Kathryn's answer machine who listened to her messages in the early hours of the morning.

Kathryn had said, once, 'I don't do hospitals.' Erin laughed at the time. Later, when she waited in the car park for the coffee and painkillers to kick in before the drive home, the phrase echoed round her head. I don't do hospitals, she repeated to herself. I don't do hospitals. Who does? Even her mother, who stayed in one long enough to know the names of all the nurses on her ward, wanted to go home as soon as possible. Home, in the end, was Erin's single bed in her Hackney flat; Erin slept on the sofa, when she managed to sleep at all.

Her mother used to say, on the days she was feeling better, 'Why don't you go out? I can manage.' But Erin didn't want to go out. She was too lonely to go outside into the world of other people's friendships.

*

In Russia, smiling is considered insincere, possibly even dangerous. Superfluous smiling is a mark of a spy, or someone who wants to trick you out of your money. This information, provided by a cheap travel guide, comforted Erin, who hadn't felt like smiling in a long time. The taut, suspicious faces of their fellow passengers created the perfect setting for Erin's soul-searching. No distractions. No small-talk. Just the mnemonic sound of the train rolling on the tracks. And the tundra speeding past in its yawning monotony. Most of the time, she slept, and every time she woke, she looked forward to sleeping again.

'God I'm bored.' Kathryn swung her feet from the top bunk. 'I'll go get tea, shall I? And where's that woman with lunch?'

As she climbed down, she accidentally kicked Erin's books from the folding table. Standing with her hands on her hips, she dominated the space.

'Here you go,' Kathryn said, coming back with two steaming cups of hot water. 'Well,' she continued. 'Aren't you drinking the tea I made?'

'Not now.'

'Waiting until it's cold, is it?'

'Later.' Erin turned to face the wall, hugging her knees to her chest. She felt her friend's eyes on her back.

'Erin.'

'I want to sleep for a bit longer.'

'Erin, seriously, that's all you do.' She heard Kathryn slump onto the seat. The silence grew tense. She sensed Kathryn deliberating whether to give up or go on.

'Are you alright?' Kathryn managed.

'Yes.' Erin reluctantly opened her eyes. The slats on the bunk above were covered in graffiti.

'Well,' said Kathryn. 'If you're sure.'

'Really, I'm fine. I just need to rest.'

'Are you annoyed with me?'

'Annoyed?'

Kathryn had come to the funeral. Every time Erin feels she might be brave enough to talk about the betrayal, she has to remember that day. At the wake, Erin locked herself in her room and refused to go downstairs. It was the sudden arrival of all those people she hadn't seen in so long. Relatives who'd failed to visit her mother when she was most desperate. The aunts and uncles and Kathryn too: she wanted to tell them all, you're too late! You should have seen her when she was alive, not now she's dead. The anger translated into a fit of coughing and crying. She ran to her room and threw herself on her bed as if she was thirteen again. The smell of coffee and toast from downstairs pervaded the room. Kathryn knocked on her door, tried to persuade her to come eat. Erin continued to sob, her head buried in a pillow. Kathryn knelt down and stroked her hair. Please come downstairs, she said. At the sound of her voice, which was uncharacteristically soft and quiet, Erin looked up. Kathryn's dark skin was flushed red, her eyelashes wet, and a line of snot hung from her left nostril. She wiped it with the back of her hand. Come downstairs. Erin obeyed. It was a long time since she'd seen Kathryn cry. The two women washed their faces and sat on the edge of the bath together, preparing themselves. Kathryn held Erin's hand. I still have the set of watercolours she gave me when we were on holiday, do you remember? Erin nodded. I was nine years old. She showed me how to use them. How much paint to water. We were in Cornwall and the first thing I painted was the sea. Kathryn spent the rest of the afternoon close by, touching Erin's arm, the small of her back, lightly, comfortingly. She helped her through awkward conversations, steered her away from people she didn't want to see. In that single afternoon of the wake, Erin was so grateful to her friend she almost forgave her everything.

'Well? Are you annoyed with me?' Kathryn repeated.

'I'm not.'

'I notice you don't speak to me anymore.' Kathryn's expression was tired, melancholic.

'Really?' Erin managed.

'If you didn't want me to come, you should have said...'

There was a knock on the compartment door. The cook appeared with the polystyrene boxes. It smelled strongly of boiled fish.

'I'm starving,' said Erin quickly, opening her lunch. Inside, the fish's flesh was yellow. Peas floated in a green pool of water.

'Disgusting,' said Kathryn, tossing it to one side. 'I can't wait until we get some real food.'

Without speaking, the passengers of the Rossiya prepare themselves for the onward journey; the cook kicks her cigarette stub under the train. The waitress rises slowly from her squat. Passengers stamp their feet, brush the biscuit crumbs from their jackets, alighting in silence, like a procession of solemn choirboys. And the conductor, like a priest bestowing his benediction, holds up his right forefinger. One minute left.

Erin's heart beats rapidly; her pacing grows frenetic. There is still no sign of Kathryn. She walks back and forth, back and forth, skirting the edges of the platform. The dark is impenetrable.

The conductor raises a stern finger again. One minute.

'Wait!' she cries. 'We're missing someone!'

He lowers his arm. The ghost of his pale finger remains suspended in the darkness. There is no arguing with Moscow time.

Erin spins around and begins to scream. She is so loud, so wild, she can hardly hear her own voice. Blood pumps in her ears. The baby starts to cry again, but Erin's screams drown it out:

'KATHRYN!'

Her thoughts race through possible scenarios: a flickering picture book of horror. She sees herself alone on the train: safe and warm, her passport in hand. I must get on the train, she thinks. I have to leave her. Then another image: Kathryn alone on the platform, desperately beating at the windows; Kathryn attacked, weeping, beaten, robbed in some lightless cell; Kathryn on the street with nothing, anonymous and abandoned. And Erin imagines herself, profile illuminated in the train window, calmly waving goodbye.

Panic transforms into a prickling pain, running down her

42

arms and legs. She sobs breathlessly. Oh god, what if she's dead? She whispers, I can't lose another one.

A whistle slices through her cries. People are laughing at her from the train. Someone shouts, mimicking, 'Kathryn! Kathryn!' in a high-pitched voice, making faces through the window.

'Kathryn,' she murmurs.

Finally, as the conductor moves to lock the carriage door, Kathryn returns. She pulls herself up onto the platform, towards the piercing light of the train. She extends an arm, and Erin catches it, and they are children again, clutching each other in the close dark of a long sleepover.

Natalie Ann Holborow
(First Prize)

Blood Sugar

The incidence of type 1 diabetes in the UK has doubled every 20 years since 1945 (Source: JDRF)

A spoonful of sugar with the medicine
and I'm sicker than before.
I feel my way to the bathroom
to drown. It's a fucking joke –
blood sugar –
life is sweet, my body
a barrel of water, still dying
of thirst, squatting skinny-legged
to piss for the twentieth time tonight.
Suck the cold tap in a sweat.

I was eight years old and vanishing.
I must have been vanishing, I thought then,
looking back at my own eyes
dark as pansies, knees awkward
as doorknobs in saggy leggings.
Christmas on tinseled wards.
The tenth door of my advent calendar
swung open to reveal me

bony and awkward on a starched white bed
and learned *phlebotomy* was a bloody word.
I feared the nurse, her stub-nailed,
soap-smell rub, snapping her rubber fingers.
I writhed in reptilian hands, tourniquets,
as she gently pushed up my sleeve
to expose a thin arm. Broke the news after lunch.

There is a bruise on my leg
like a tiny and squashed violet.
My handbag is a scatter of lipsticks,
receipts with Fruit Pastilles stuck
between them in sticky kisses,
the sting of loose needles, a lifeline.

Bite

I. Snow White

I laid their linen
   in dwarfish squares,
   heart breaking for these poor lambs
abandoned in a thatched cottage,
   pulling the sheets
   with seven pairs of hands
and no mother to kiss their fingers.
   Feeling regal almost,
   I sit before these china cups,
butter-knives, scrubbed little spoons
   upon the tea-ringed table,
   scoop cold berries from the bowl
and later, bored with searching
   for little boys,
   float up the staircase to bed
in a spiral of dust-motes,
   making my shadow known.
   The children are on their way home now
while I warm a small bed with my body,
   but gasping and fished
   from a whirlpool of dreams,
I wake to Adam's apples.

II. The Wicked Queen

It was only natural she should
    fall in love
    with the fat sweet heart
of a bad apple, what with her
    being so young
    and lustful –
trophied in sexual fantasies –
    the dreaming adolescent prince
    sweats like a pig,
white visions
    of her slim wrist turning the handle,
    revealing herself baby-eyed
to the whistle of seven men.
    He can lie back now
to his heart's content,
    one eye unpeeled,
    sobbing and breathless –
sputtering into his hand
    while she goes on unbreathing,
    tucked against herself.
The red-skirted rose, her long-dead
    claim to fame –
    fairest in the land
so my mirror confirms,
    smiling at the globes
    of these queenly breasts
not even a king could resist.
    See how his visions
    circle like planets
where finding me here, irresistible,
    old enough to have raised him,
    my pale eyes intrude

on his clammy dreams,
    as the morning turns,
    spilling its blood-lights,
and rolls through forbidden orchards.

III. The Huntsman

It was then I found myself
    towering above her, throwing my axe,
    a priest in bloody worship
before the trembling lamb.
    I'll never forget the brilliance
    of a milkwhite face,
the snowcapped curve of her shoulders,
    where her dress slipped
    and revealed too much of her
in a cage of lean firs,
    mouth open – her horror
at seeing a man with a weapon.
    Lips wide, hair black
    as the gleaming eel,
I looked away, took a deep breath
    while butterflies shut
    in their thousands –
yet choked by her perfume,
    circled by birds,
    I left her to hunt the boars.

IV. Prince Charming

I found her passed out in the forest.
    Surrounded by males all sniffing their griefs,

I muscled in between them –
'*Charming*,' one told me, fists curled.
     I nodded hello to the little thug,
     leaned down upon my princess
and kissed her without thinking,
     having travelled too far
     and much too long,
alone amongst fallen apples.
     Perhaps it was true love
     or the nip of my incisors
that raised her then from the dead –
     yawning, her small mouth
     said nothing,
but riding away, girl cleaved to my side,
     I gave her a fairytale ending.

Vinegar

It was Jack's sixth Sunday of being a saint.

'Delyth's cooking Sunday dinner,' said Dan, leaning out through the back door to let the cat in. He watched Delyth's cardiganed shape move through the steamy windows, the sound of her Madonna CD and her four bickering children drifting across the garden, carried by the smell of roast lamb and mashed swede.

'Good for Delyth,' Jack said, elbow-deep in the freezer. His denimed backside stuck out, wiggling as he scrabbled among the boxes of fish fingers and value-range pizzas.

Dan frowned. 'Why don't we ever have a Sunday dinner?'

'I haven't got time to piss about with roasting no dinners, Dan.'

'Well what are we having?'

'Dunno.' Jack tugged out a box of ancient chicken kievs, sending a shower of flaked ice to the tiles like electrical sparks. 'These with chips?'

'No.'

'Well what then?'

'Sunday dinner.'

'Dan, I don't have nothing for no Sunday bloody dinner.' He slammed the box to the worktop and pulled a bag of potatoes from the cupboard. 'You'll appreciate what you're given.'

'How very Christian of you,' said Dan, watching as his father took a handful of potatoes to the sink and scrubbed the earthy skins under a blast of tapwater. He yawned. Fair play to Jack, he'd kept up this charade a lot longer than Dan had predicted. Dan would have bet his last fiver that his father would have given up and found himself slipping out of the off-licence with a four-pack of lager under his coat within a fortnight. Six weeks in and he was still going strong, a Saint Christopher dripping gold from his neck.

'I don't know what your problem is,' muttered Jack, peeling potato skins. His face looked old in the dirty light that sliced through the blinds, his skin stretched over his cheeks like pale leather. He didn't always look like that – old and sad. He used to draw looks from the mothers at the school gate, huddled together like hens in their rain coats, their beady eyes swinging towards him. They smiled and smiled over their scarves. Jack Jenkins cut quite a figure, towering above the other parents and stretching his broad arms to embrace the boy flinging himself at his Daddy, his hero at the school gates.

They'd been to church that morning. Jack Jenkins had actually dragged his son to *church*. Dan had noticed Jack's palms pressed together just above his crotch halfway through the service, as though he could pray in secret. Actually pressed together, like he thought himself some saint – Jack, with that wine-coloured scar snaking down his jaw and that oversized corduroy jacket that stank of rolled tobacco and wet dog. He used to hide whole bottles of whiskey in that jacket, just walk around in the middle of the day down the Kingsway with a bottle of cheap booze clinking against his rib, and then sit at the side of the train station slugging it. He'd spend hours there, eyes rolling as the shadows leaned darker and longer over the traffic, scraping loose pennies towards him with a grubby finger and throwing cold chips

51

at the seagulls. Sometimes Muggs came to join him, a pack of cards whispering between his hands.

And he thought the Bible could save him. The *Bible*. A stinking, grubby, useless, boring, pile-of-shit *book* was going to turn him into a new man. Jack Jenkins, the shiny new, squeaky-clean do-gooder who worried about things like poverty and praying for sick people in hospitals and abandoned kids and all the crap that none of them could do anything about.

Dan passed his eyes over his father's faded polo-neck and the denim jeans hanging loose from his bony hips. If Mam could see him now, she'd have curled her lip and spat.

'All you ever used to do was go on at me to get clean. On and on and on. You and your mother,' Jack said, lifting his eyes to the window above the sink. His face hardened. 'Ashamed of your old man, that's what you said.'

'...Well, yeah. No one wants to point out that the bloke spewing against the train station wall is their old man, do they?'

'So what the hell am I doing wrong by staying off it then?' Jack threw down the peeler and turned to look at his son. A vein wriggled down to meet the long scar, pearlescent in the afternoon light. 'Huh? What am I doing wrong? Wrong now for a man to have a bit of faith in something other than a can of fucking lager? Want me to tell you to stick a fucking curry in the microwave while I go down the club all evening? Huh? Do you?' He laughed. 'Maybe I'll bump into Muggs, have a few for old times' sake.'

Dan dropped his gaze. They never talked about Muggs.

'Here.' Jack rooted in his back pocket and cradled a handful of pound coins in his palm. 'Go down the shop and get some vinegar, will you?' He slammed the cupboard door. 'We've run out.'

They were already outside the rugby club when he passed, brows crumpled against the sunlight and cigarettes skewed from their lips.

The Boys. They watched Dan shuffle past with his earphones in, glancing up at them from beneath his hood. Paul gave him a stiff nod, drumming his fingers on his beer belly, a fat sovereign on his ring finger. The men muttered to each other in low voices, moving their lips only slightly as though Dan couldn't see. An explosion of laughter boomed out from the huddle as four pairs of eyes followed him down the road. Dan turned his music up. Bastards.

Every building was the colour of an ashtray. It didn't matter how bright the April sun burned against the terraced houses, every shop front and squashed little home sulked in perpetual gloom, spitting out human shapes and little dogs every now and then or blowing out plumes of smoke through kitchen windows. Sunday afternoon: the whole street smelled of gravy.

Albert's Stores stood at the end of the street, marked by a faded sign and a group of teens wheeling about on bikes outside the door, cans of Red Bull in their fists.

'Alright,' Dan said, nodding at their ringleader. The lanky boy nodded back.

Dan stepped into the cramped little shop, a jumble of overpriced tins, speckled bananas dangling from hooks and a messy display of newspapers strewn across the racks. The whole shop smelled of paper and old carpets. A lottery machine sputtered somewhere from behind the counter as Dan ducked behind the shelves, walled by rows of out-of-date biscuits and tatty rolls of giftwrap. He picked up a bottle of vinegar, slipped to the back of the store and found himself among the envelopes and stationery. He thought about his father's twitching fingers before Albert moved the whiskey behind the counter to stop him grabbing it.

Dan don't know why he did it. His hand closed around a pot of markers.

Sidling up to the counter, Dan paid for the bottle of vinegar. Albert eyed him conspicuously, a row of gold-coloured liquors glittering behind him on the shelf.

'That father of yours staying out of trouble?' he asked, looking at Dan down his long nose. He reminded Dan of a crow, dressed in dark turtlenecks and arms lifting like wings whenever he reached for the cigarettes.

Dan frowned, rubbing a five-pound note between his thumb and forefinger. 'None of your business.'

Albert's eyebrows floated upwards, a small smirk curling on his lip. 'Carry on with that attitude and you'll be out of here as well.'

'And these.' Dan slid a packet of fizzy sweets over the counter.

'Sixty pence.'

'That's no way to ask.'

'Did you hear what I said? You want to be banned as well?' Albert leaned over the counter. 'What have you got in those pockets of yours, eh?'

'What?'

'Go on. Empty your pockets.'

'You can't just accuse me.'

'I know you've got something in there.' Albert narrowed his eyes. 'Just like that drunken father of yours –'

'Fuck you.'

Albert swooped at him. 'Empty your bloody pockets!'

Dan ran. He ran and ran through Emlyn Street, past the grey-faced houses, tearing past the rugby club and nearly colliding with Big Delyth chasing the cat out of the garden. He ran right past his house.

Panting, he stopped and gripped the railings of the iron fence that surrounded Fairfield Park like a cage, the children crawling in and out of tunnels like rats on the jungle gym. What the hell was he doing? He pushed his hair back with a clammy hand, bent double and sucked in the cold spring air. A small boy eyed him from underneath the climbing frame, his face pale and a scrub of ginger hair springing from his skull. He looked too small to be alone, crouched there in his scruffy parka and popping crisps into his babyish mouth.

He'd forgotten the vinegar.

The boy tucked his knees up to his chest as Dan passed him to sit among the smashed glass on the tarmac, a bottle-green constellation beneath the swings. He pulled out the bundle of markers tied up with a rubber band in his hoody pocket. What the hell did he want to nick five shitty marker pens for? He slid one out of the rubber band and popped off the lid. God, he loved that smell. He tried it against his hand, but nothing came out; just a weak smudge dragged across his knuckles. Face hardening, he stabbed the nib at the ground and tossed it across the field. The little boy followed it with his eyes.

He did the same with the second. And the third. The fourth left a thick black line across his fist. Smiling, he carried it over to the stone wall that divided the church grounds from the playground. On both sides of the wall, cigarette ends and faded pink crisp packets fluttered against the weeds that clustered either side. God, this place was ugly, even in the sun. Even the trees looked exhausted. Behind him, the boy crept up to watch him, dropping to crouch behind the metal slide. He chewed slowly on a mouthful of crisps.

Dan wrote his name. He didn't know why. Then he wrote his name again. He wrote his name over and over, *Daniel Daniel Daniel Daniel*, until the letters became meaningless scribbles and the words started to look strange, a nestful of snakes crawling over the stones. Stained-glass Jesus gleamed above him, darker this side of the window. *You can talk to Jesus*, the Reverend had said once, gripping the rosary around his neck. *Talk to him and talk to the Father*. How the hell would Jesus understand? He was alright – his father was always right where he was supposed to be: everywhere, all the time, and he didn't even have a body to carry him around. There were times when Jack couldn't have dragged his whiskey-sodden body to the bathroom for a piss.

He turned to the little boy beneath the slide. 'You want a go?' Dan asked him, offering him the other marker. The boy shrank back. Dan shrugged. 'Suit yourself.'

Daniel Daniel Daniel. Daniel Edwyn Jenkins. He never told anyone his middle name. He was named after his grandfather, who he couldn't really remember apart from a brown waistcoat and a red Bible on his bedside table, a soft old cheek smelling of tobacco and that terrible phlegmy cough that still came to him if he tried hard enough to think about it. He'd died of emphysema when Dan turned four. That was probably the first time Dan had noticed the cider cans over the coffee table and the shouting and his mother's disappearing off into the night a year later. Then the vodka bottles moved in, filling the spaces left by Mam's belongings and Muggs came to haunt the kitchen late at night with his pack of cards, grinning with cigarettes clamped between his teeth.

The boy tiptoed up beside him, his nose smeared with snot, leaving a thin yellow crust above his mouth. He stretched out his hand for the marker pen. Dan handed it to him without smiling.

The boy popped off the lid with tiny fingers and frowned at the wall.

'Like this.' Dan wrote across the stones: *Daniel Edwyn Jenkins*. The little boy copied him, word for word, his letters tall and wobbly. Dan laughed. 'Is your name Daniel Edwyn Jenkins?'

The little boy shook his head.

'Then write your name. Not mine.'

The boy lifted his pen again. His parka was definitely a couple of sizes too big for him, the sleeves swallowing his hands whole. He pushed the cuffs back and pressed the pen nib to the wall, concentrating hard. His tongue poked out and slid along his lips as he wrote, a pink little blade. He stepped back and blinked at the black letters drying onto the stones. Dan stared at the boy's handiwork.

'Boy?' Dan dropped down onto his haunches, levelling his height with the kid's. 'Your name is Boy?'

The boy nodded.

'That's a funny name.' Behind them, the kids slowly succumbed to the calls of their parents. One girl squealed, announcing that she was going for ice cream with her Daddy. The sound of hard footballs against rubber soles kicked away across the field, leaving only a scattering of crows cawing and pecking at the crumbs left behind on the tarmac. 'Is that a nickname?'

Boy took up the pen and wrote again. *Boy. Boy Boy Boy Boy.*

'Do you have a second name then?'

Boy looked up at Dan, confused.

'Did your parents ever tell you why they chose that name?' Dan asked him. Boy shook his head. 'What do the teachers call you?'

Boy wrote it again. *Boy*.

Dan lifted himself up to his full height as a man called out from behind the railings.

'Are you listening?' A red face the shape of a full moon scowled out from beneath a knitted hat, a cigarette clamped between his teeth. 'Get your arse over here boy if you know what's good for you. You're coming in.' The man blew a stream of grey against the sky and grinned as Dan turned to face him. He'd recognise that grin and wax jacket anywhere.

'Well well well, *shw'mae bach.*' He laughed, a cruel wheezing laugh forcing its way up from his lungs. 'Oh, sorry. Do I say *God bless* now?'

Dan's fists tightened around the pens.

'Y'know, I'll give him two months. Two months and he's gonna cave.' Muggs put his hand to his right pocket, as he always did, to check his cards were still there. 'You really think he's gonna sit there in that miserable living room with a cup of fucking tea when the internationals are on?' He snorted and flung the cigarette butt to the floor. 'Bollocks. He ain't gonna stay in and watch telly on his own. Internationals, it's tradition. He'll tell you, *just one pint see, it's the rugby.* He'll be rat-arsed after one sniff of booze. Still...you could always pray for him.'

Dan shook. What he'd have given to knock Muggs's few remaining teeth into the back of his throat.

'C'mon, boy.' Muggs set his jaw and frowned at the tiny boy behind Dan's legs. 'You're coming in. Stick a DVD on or something, go to bed when you're tired. Consider yourself bloody lucky, boy...ain't many kids can say they're allowed to stay up late as they want and have free reign of the fucking house.'

Boy dropped his head and followed his father out of the gate.

'You been writing on them walls?' Muggs jerked his head at the church walls. Boy shrugged. 'Little shit. And you,' he turned to Dan, 'you should know better. Not very holy, vandalising the fucking church.' He wheezed a laugh and walked away, gripping his son by the arm and coughing violently.

Dan watched him go. Behind him, Jesus could have been waving after them over an old man's head.

Jack would be waiting for his vinegar.

Claire Houguez
(Highly Commended)

Within the Yellow Plumage

I'm supposed to be keeping my mind in the moment but it keeps wandering off, crossing borders.

Where am I now? Part of the overspill of tables and fraying wicker seats of a tiny fast food outlet, feet tucked into the angled shadow of a narrow awning. Passers-by occasionally brush the edge of the table with handbags or sleeves as they drift down the narrow street, peer sideways into the open notebook in front of me.

Every day Livia leaves me post-it notes containing landmarks to meet her at after work, tempting me further and further away from the few blocks of Tokyo that I've mapped so far. While I'm waiting it's more comfortable to pull out my journal than to people watch as I would at home. Here, curious glances are met with the shock of mutual eye contact – I am equally novel. Instead I'm savouring inked versions of the words that mull around my mouth every day: *arigatou, sumimasen, onigiri*. But I also find myself writing of home, of the things I no longer have to return to.

Livia's copper head appears further down the street. She is gracile in a pencil skirt and bowed neck-scarf, eyes lowered, satchel swinging. She arrives at the table, slings her bag into the wicker opposite and asks if I'd like another drink. I watch through the window as she enters the burger joint, becomes opaque and greyed, scanning the mysterious characters on the walls, speaking confidently to the sales assistant.

Livia upped and moved to Japan as my other friends were slowly and surely disappearing into marriage. The girls I'd drunk gin out of teacups with, in the early hours of the morning, now wanted to talk mortgages, bailed on work drinks to cook elaborate dinners for their 'partners' (when did they graduate from *boyfriends*?). Chicken with brie wrapped in bacon, adorned with parsley. Of course I didn't notice so much until Ian left me.

After weeks of hushed, you-can-tell-us, *How's it all goings,* I loved answering with the news I was spontaneously upping sticks to Japan to stay with Livia. The look on their faces. I'd say 'I'm sure I can sort everything at the airport,' carefully carefree for extra shock value, and their faces went like when I used to tell people I was a burlesque dancer; it reminded me of a time I did more than come home from work and watch soaps on the sofa, bland soup du jour rotating in the kitchen beside the mouldering dishes and unopened bank statements.

Livia returns with two iced green teas, bitterness anticipated with cartons of gum syrup. She nods at my journal as she settles the tray, approving of it, as she does of my desire to submerge myself in this city, sluice my cells with something different. The journal has swelled with receipts, leaflets, tourist maps and train tickets, proof that I am here, experiencing something. On the thick, lineless pages, jubilant descriptions of calligraphy, pandas, ikebana, new experiences sandwiched between snippets of existing memory. The stuff that pours out of my pen when I'm not actively distracted by other things.

Livia begins a conversation about the relationship history of Adele and Christian, who will be joining us tonight for the burlesque show. Why on earth did I suggest it? How will I explain myself if I get upset in front of Livia's friends?

'It's so complicated getting laid in Japan,' Livia sighs without the merest hint of dissatisfaction.

We were having dinner with Livia's friends – urban bohemians, loud with the swelled confidence of an up-cycled living space. They persuaded us down a back road in Kitazawa, up a steep flight of stairs into a blur of strip-lighting and echoes of 'Irasshaimase!' The only table left was a *tatami*. Livia's stage-whisper – 'Emma, slip your shoes off here' – as we reached the shoe-strewn step annoyed me. In Tokyo I am an understudy without a script, and every blunder – standing in the wrong place, talking too loudly on the train – results in the other characters staring at me, not to mention sniggers from the audience.

Livia carefully knelt at the *tatami*, smoothing her skirt over her bunched thighs and sitting serenely, back straight; Adele settled into a tilted mermaid and I lumbered down opposite, drawing my knees up to my chest. Drinks appeared and the talk moved evenly around the table – stories about past travels and exotic experiences, shared with shrugging insouciance and peppered with bursts of brief laughter. I tried to nod and smile enough that people would think I was part of things. It's times like this I miss being a dancer, having unordinary stories of my own to share.

The waiter spooned cabbage in a milky sauce on to a hot rectangle in the centre of the table, returning at intervals to fashion the mixture into three hollows, breaking an egg into each; sprinkling shellfish, spices and bacon, folding the thickened parcels in on themselves. As Adele asked 'What shall we do tomorrow?' I was sure she already had something in mind but I found myself jumping in: 'Why don't we see if there's a burlesque night?'

Intrigued, the group began to check for a listing on their phones. It so happened that a night in Shibuya was found and slowly translated. Livia dropped into the conversation that 'Emma used to be a burlesque performer' and I was suddenly the subject of genuine interest.

Christian asked, 'How can you do it? Get up there in front of so many people?' and I found myself answering as I always do – did – 'Because the thought of *not* doing it is more terrifying!'

Later on, Adele asked 'Why did you stop?' through a mouthful of pancake-omelette. I'd been talking burlesque up so much that I paused, wasn't sure how to explain. Fortunately the painstaking translation and divvying up of the shared bill had begun and I said 'excuse me a second', and pretended I wasn't sure how many notes I needed.

We nip back to Livia's apartment on our way to the station to freshen up. It smells of the dregs of sober tea. It's so muggy that my cells have swelled, making my clothing constrictive.

I can hear the clack of clothes hangers up in the sleeping area as Livia tries dresses and puts them back again. I try to victory roll my hair in the bathroom, winding it around my fingers, elbows knocking against the walls. The sweat-wet strands refuse to be coaxed away from my scalp and the resulting pin curls are drooping, lopsided. I shove in some flowers to disguise the worst of it, colour in my brows and fumble a quick cupid's bow in red lipstick – my made-up face familiarly strange – as I hear Livia clopping towards me.

In Tokyo, the sound of birdsong is played as the trains wait in stations. We jump on the Inokashira line. The women in the carriage are layered with scarves, cardigans, but appear cool. My neck is damp under the silk scarf carefully hiding my décolletage. Every so often my gaze falls on someone who is already eyeing me. I compose a sentence for my journal: *the flowers pull against their hairpins and the make-up feels loud on my skin; it's strange to be stared at again on terms that I'm used to.*

An old woman leans across, breath sourly alcoholic, to ask, 'Where are you from?'

Livia bristles. 'Kitazawa', she says, tersely, then quietly, to me, 'If I stay here ten years they'll still ask me that'. Then, 'Japanese women aren't supposed to drink Saki.'

Livia has been here for a year now and it suits her. Here, she seems well-dressed, rather than conservative, respectful, rather than mousey. I think she'd like to settle here if only she wouldn't always be a foreigner. As we leave the train, she nudges me, points out a group of Sweet Lolitas making their way across the platform for the line to Harajuku, dressed in puffed-out gingham, their multi-coloured hair teased huge, adorned with bows. They chatter and giggle as they clop along, feet turned in, calves straining, in shoes purposely too big.

'*Ah Kawaii*,' says Adele loudly, snorting.

We pay more than we expect to for the show, file in. It's already started and the lights are dimmed. The only free table is near the front and we mime tiptoeing to get to it. On the chairs are flyers for upcoming performances and classes. Across the table, Christian is pointing out a listing for boylesque among the advertised workshops. Adele snort-shrugs her disbelief. I slip the show receipt into my journal.

On stage a group of performers sit around a table, seem to be discussing the evening ahead. Livia turns in her chair to whisper a translation to me. I lean forward expectantly, hear: 'They're talking so fast, I don't know what they are saying!' There is a great deal of laughter. Livia manages: 'The women are talking about the time they went to Paris, to the Crazy Horse, how the dancers all had legs up to here... how they can't compete, as Japanese women… how they've had to find their own way to be sexy.'

When the dancing begins, despite the neon bobbed wigs and the playful wash of colour and glitter, I find that the Japanese burlesque dancers don't camp up the striptease aspect like we do at home – signalling the striptease elements clearly, making a meal of it. The dancers are all drilled to perfection, in time with clear lines, but every movement is also infused with joy. Watching the Tokyo performers, my body begins to twitch.

The compere's mysterious flow of dialogue is interrupted again and again by the word 'showtime', but soon he spreads his fingers, palm out, for the last time. The final act. A ripple of appreciation draws me to the back of the room. A profusely yellow shape is making its slow way through the tables, a woman enclosed in large fans, matching feathered headdress bobbing. Within the yellow plumage is a harvest moon of a face, a purple bobbed wig, lavish red lips. There's a calm stolidity to her bearing and she takes several minutes to reach the stage, where she turns, allowing us the full effect of the encircling feathers under the lighting. One fan is held vertically behind her back, one pressed in front, feathers meeting in a sparse canopy down the edges of her ribs. The fans are thick with Ostrich feathers, lightly rhinestoned along the stems; I can tell from here that they're expensive, weighty, though her wrist movements are light.

Facing away from the audience, she flicks both fans outwards – revealing skin zigzagged with glittering yellow straps – and sweeps them back. Beside me, Livia and Christian are cooing, but, as a traditional sequence of fan moves ensues – her wrists sending them spinning around her one by one, front always covered – I wonder if this is going to be yet another self-indulgent, repetitive fan routine. The kind I started to notice more and more as my disillusionment grew.

Safe in the dimly-lit seats, I allow my face to set into disappointment.

Ian stopped coming to the shows a year or so in, said he'd seen enough routines, that they'd all blurred into sameness. I didn't push him on it, I hadn't come up with new routines myself in a while anyway, in the snatched time between nine to five and all the travelling. I didn't go along to any shows that I wasn't dancing in, caught bits of other routines in the wings, compared costumes, cheers, started to feel ground down by the whole thing.

The yellow-plumed dancer dips down from the stage, into the front row of the audience, eyes lowered, encircled once more in a sideways, feathered oyster shell. She pauses, drops her gaze and a royal blue wash of lighting picks out eyelashes heavily flashed with gold. Making her way along the first line of seats, she lifts her lashes for chosen audience members, pulsing the feathers open and closed as she does so, drawing noisy approval from the front row. Livia and Christian crane their necks to see and I find myself joining them.

As the music begins to wind down, she returns to the stage and, facing away, once more stretches out the fans to their fullest capacity. Turning, slowly, she reveals a bump, six months gone. As the audience erupt, she drops the feathers to frame it, and her face relaxes into joy.

As the plane climbs away from Narita airport, we pass through one of those beams of light that show up in the clouds of Old Masters' paintings – a spray of gold across the grey backs of the seats in front: a final burst of auspicious-feeling magic.

As we level, shutters begin to close throughout the plane; people get cosy under blankets, plug into the in-flight movies. I wrestle my journal out of the netting on the chair-back in front of me, wanting to wrap up neatly the last few days of the trip. As the plane flies over Siberia I crack open the shutter to peep out, letting a wash of white light into the cabin, brighter than a spotlight.

When I began burlesque I wanted to be the next Dita von Teese, parading like a showgirl, dripping rhinestones. But when I got on stage I found that I capered, tried to disarm people, win them over. I couldn't quite manage to emulate the serious sensuousness of the professional performers. The ones that didn't ask for applause, expected it. I watched their sound-checks, as they mimed their routines in jeans, winking and nodding at imaginary audience members. I'd get my make-up and costume on early enough to angle myself in the wings so I could mark their accents, the way they set up a catalyst and coaxed a response from the front rows. I went all over the country attending workshops by famous dancers, dragged my case around performing for five years – with late night phone calls to Ian from cheap hotel rooms, peeling off my eyelashes and pasties in bed, trying to muster the energy for phone sex between rough sheets.

My confidence on stage began to improve, but I found it hard to make the transition from newcomer to professional around full-time work. I was too tired backstage to network other performers, stopped watching the other sound checks. At home, I sat up late mending costumes while Ian slept, applying for shows, practising routines crab-like in the strip of kitchen – losing gloves into the hanging saucepans and bras into cupboards. I missed weddings, christenings, anniversaries, finding my own way back from the station on Sunday evenings to a silent flat, half-empty pizza boxes. And though, for that eight minutes I was on stage in a show, the blood-fizz and the ringing cheers made my skin glow, it began to seem just that bit too hard the rest of the time. I began to wonder if it was worth it.

It never occurred to me that Ian would be unfaithful – I

would have said once, what woman would try to compete with a burlesque dancer? He'd mentioned her a few times, casually, in passing. I'd seen her in photos of staff dos. Nothing special. Not like me, glamorous, travelling around, making a name for myself.

I heard through mutual friends a few months ago that Ian and Emily were pregnant – I hate the way people say that, that the *couple* is pregnant. I wonder how far along she is now. I would have given him a child eventually. I'd thought it was a case of burlesque or baby.

The old Japanese woman next to me chuckles when I order *onigari* from the hostess, and she a packet of ham sandwiches. She ignores the open journal, the unwritten rule, wants to tell me about the sightseeing she'll be doing in England. She pulls out an Ordnance Survey booklet and I'm encouraged to trace my time in the UK with my fingertip for her: where I went to school, to university, where I live now and, unmentioned, I trace where I lived with Ian, all the cities I have performed in. As we drop into London, a swirl of grey rain surrounds us. I say, 'Welcome to Britain' but she doesn't laugh. As people begin gathering things from the overhead lockers, she hands me her paper fan, says 'I don't think I'll need this. You have it.'

I will keep the fan in my bag, a token. Perhaps I will find a way to use it in the new act that has begun to bud in my mind – closed petals slowly ringing with colour – whenever I think of the funny walk of the Harajuku girls, the reveal of the bump. Whenever I remember that there's more I haven't yet explored.

Lucy Ann Jones
(Commended)

Table Set for Two

Thirty-one, young, lives in that perfect house
on the hill by the river. Call me
for a messy smile in the mornings,
for dancing, pub lunches and more.

Looking for similar girls,
for support, cups of tea at 1am,
for what was lost through high school,
for dancing, pub lunches and more.

Will eat whatever you want, if you
tell me I look good in red,
tell me it suits my skin, for the everyday,
for dancing, pub lunches and more.

Our arguments won't be too long,
we might not sleep in the same bed
but you'll get to work on time, and I'll still go
for dancing, pub lunches and more.

Thirty one years, lives in that
broken house on the hill, by the river.
Call me for a smile in the mornings,
for dancing, pub lunches and more.

The Parade

saw you, in the parade wednesday autumn night
ddddddddruuumsssss and streamed streamers turningstreet
red, washed blue and red
band hats stacked twice your height, galled, face, laced with
ginger braid
the bassdrums on beatmy pound myheart
pou nd pound myheart

ddddddddruuumsssss and streamed streamers turningstreet
red, washed blue and red
you swallow applause with every step
every march stepped
the bassdrums on beatmy pound myheart
pou nd pound myheart
skin on skin on sunsoaked trombones you are 1 of 1000 to
everyonebutme

you swallow applause with every step
every march stepped
bam bam ba-ahm. bam bam smi-le gir-ls smi-le
skin on skin on sunsoaked trombones you are 1 of 1000 to
everyonebutme
mary jane shoes buckles sc-cuff town street floor on the
road again

bam bam ba-ahm. bam bam smi-le gir-ls smi-le
mary jane shoes buckles sc-cuff town street floor on the
road again
saw you, in the parade wednesday autumn night
dddddddruuumsssss and streamed streamers turningstreet
red, washed blue and red

The Voyage Out
For Captain R. Fitzroy of the HMS Beagle

30th April, 1865. My home sank into vapid darkness. I sensed something hanging from every rafter, never quick enough to see who, or what, but I felt the unbearable draft as they swung. There was a constant banging on my door those days. A mother, a sister, howling me down, pushing their fist through the bitten wood to point their fingers at me. I was the reason for their husband's burial at sea. Their cause of death listed as Fitzroy's pathetic trials in forecasting. As if I were the divine power behind the ocean, not merely its foreign translator.

'If only,' I mumbled aloud. 'If only I had been gifted something for being the children's villain. The Captain of bloody seas.'

By this date, I'd suffered a horrid dip into a severe illness. Not of physical limbs or organs, but of thoughts. Every moment outside the threshold of my home was what I could only predict our Hell was like. I don't blame him, Charles. If not him, it would have been someone else. He is a good man, continues to be. Suffered through me, my order, my iron fist, for his belief. To measure up cowardly to such a figure is what weighs down my shoulders every morning, I believe.

The entirety of my house stank of charcoal, and though I'd given up smoking, every wall was aflame. Each evening,

I'd let my eyes finally close, and walk, once more, down each and every street of all New Zealand, climbing over burning effigies of my own body. My home had become my own personal morbid museum.

Take a sharp left and watch, in the comfortable setting of the living room, as a man of Tory blood and bone falls on bright-eyed Darwin. I welcomed him over and over aboard my ship, satisfied I'd met a companion so unimposing, so quietly intelligent, that I could continue my work but have something, someone, to keep me drowning within myself. That was all he was good for, of course. A ridiculously inexperienced man at sea. Back out into the corridor before the room swells with salt water.

Keep your hands to yourself as you pass by the next few rooms. Peer through the doors slowly, you'd be cursed to be caught up in every rough course of tornadic conversation we'd had over dinner. The clink of cutlery landing scattered on the deck soon became the crew's nightly lullaby. I keep my head down as I pass, hearing my own voice, young, proud, hiss out every insult I lashed against Charles over those five long years of voyage.

'Do you know why you're here, Darwin?'

It's certainly not to give orders. I find myself running, echoing my own commands to only walk when aboard. I stumble, brace myself on the wall of my dressing room. I can feel the weight of my insides, every drop of liquor into my throat, every shift of breath and beat. At long, long last I realise what my predecessors must have when they chose their own ascension date; I am wasting good fuel. Something is keeping me upright and alive. Whether it be the Lord, or something beating in the heart of the Galapagos, I let out a heavy breath, exhaling every last remnant of sea air from my body.

The room hummed. Only slightly. An old shanty, something sung by the drunken crew, the night I'd let them loose. I never gave attention to the lyrics, only the volume. I believed they knew where the limit was and if they overstepped it, they were to be punished with a lashing. Charles was furious, that night. Came to my quarters, a cabin boy in tow.

I sat down.

'Captain Fitzroy. Permission talk about this?' His voice was soaked with care, but naively direct. He held the boy's arm high. He couldn't have been older than thirteen.

'I found him drinking while on duty.' The marks in the boy's paling skin blemished with infection, messy strikes down his soft arm. Charles stared at me, lowered his evidence, and ushered the boy out – an opportunity he quickly took, scattering his limbs in the direction of the door as if his soles were oiled. In spite of his youth, Darwin had been a respectable force. Not overwhelming, but genuine and honest in his work. His arguments against the productive use of those of lower classes for the lower work made wonderful complements to every dinner.

'I don't mean to state the obvious, but you gave it to them, Captain. You handed them the bottles.'

The hum settled. I leant back in the chair, now battered by time. Dips of my fingernails had ruined the cushioned arms. I felt each dip, one by one.

'*I am not a praying man, Captain Fitzroy,*' I repeat out to the dusty dressing room, slowly standing, pressing my palms hard to stave off their shiver. I looked forward, and what met me brought out a roar of laughter. '*But for you, I hope the Lord knows pity!*'

Stark opposite my old chair was a small shaving mirror, propped up on a bitten plank shelf. I caught only my blurred swaying body in the reflection from that distance away. It was the best I'd appeared in years. I strode over, swiping my shaving knife in one hand, and the hand mirror in the other.

The corners of my moustache still clung to old wax, spiked and split. I held it up, up, to hit the light, then down to the floor, to see what direction suited me. Neither were particularly catching, and neither fought for me. Looking closely, only at the glass, not the man contained within – there was a thin line, drawn while aboard the Beagle, that, when lined up correctly, cut the reflection's throat in half.

The banging on the door became a beat, a shelf of volumes clattering to the floor like sailor's shoes, and the chorus of crew rose up in my mind. I followed the direction clear cut, and fell to the floor.

> *Come all ye young fellows that follows the sea*
> *To me, way hey, blow the man down*
> *Now please pay attention and listen to me*
> *Give me some time to blow the man down.*

Richard Lewis
(Second Prize)

Work in Progress

You stand in my doorway
wrapped up like an apology.
Feet together, hair, maybe, longer.
You wear the glasses I always liked.
We stood for a moment,
the trees grow old and bald and bitter.
The cold lets itself in and when it leaves
it takes me with it.
We stood for a moment
and thought together, of course.

Later, we lay in bed and thought, of course.
You face the wall, my finger runs along
the words on your lower back,
the ink is still wet. Sheets
wrap over you like an envelope.
I wonder if I should read on,
is it even meant for me and in any case,
it's longer than a fucking Jeff Buckley song.
You say, 'I'm a work in progress.'
I say, 'We all are.'

When you leave, it's still dark.
Our formalities escape a handshake
by the thinnest of margins.
We say nothing we say
nothing.
I watch you down the path,
your dress black, blue trims,
like night rivers through the forest.
I close the door: my fingers
linger on the handle for a moment
and I say, Of course.

23:57

That first night they led me to those castle doors,
I weighed less than guilt.
Two officers flanked me like a prince.
Our footsteps on the gravel path
the only ripples in that stillness.

The grey grass swallowed every sound.
In the car park a single Fiesta shivered.
I left breadcrumbs soaked in wine
to the city below, where the new year approached
with the slow, single mind of a catastrophe.

The receptionist buzzed us in. Bored, middle-aged and bald.
I think of the boys at school, red sweaters.
Peroxide hair hanging daggers on their scalps.
And that word, a weaponised fairytale:
'You're mad you are butt, you'll end up in Cefn Coed.'

We wait. Third door from the right. The silence deepens
and matures, puts on a funeral suit. Starts drinking Scotch.
The officers are gargoyles in bright yellow and thick shoes.
Too big for their chairs. Their phones go off together. I realise
it's midnight. I hear footsteps, a heavy lock being pulled.
                                                    Nothing...

Some News

We know what is coming. It's expected.
Barely even news, a relief. Yet he pauses dramatically,
sinks to a squat, puts his hand on my knee.
He sits us all down, four to a three-seater,
since this was not news you hear cross-legged on the floor.
So, he says, I have some news. We know already.
Of course we do. I won't forget any time soon Nana
in that crisp white bed, all moisture sucked from her,
and I'm staring at what used to be her stomach, wondering
is that where it is? Purple and sticking to the surfaces like
                                                    an octopus?
There's an uneaten tub of hospital orange jelly, a white
                                                    jug of water.
Of course we know. I don't mention that I was bored.
Already I'm upstairs in my bedroom with the Nintendo
and that Super Mario Brothers level I've been stuck on
                                                    for weeks.
The castle keeps changing, you have to go an exact route
or you end up back at the start. In the corners of my
                                                    science books
I've drawn maps where I should have drawn equations
and blueprints of atoms which years later I would learn
                                                    were bullshit.

And then, the news. I am a fly in a cathedral.
He's still talking. I watch his bottom lip. He has crusts
lining it.
His teeth are yellow. I'm not getting a word. I need clues.
I'm unsure how to react. It's Christmas all over again,
my jaw rubber tired from smiling and now, what?
His eyes are large and expecting. I look to the left:
they certainly appear on the cusp of crying.
They are water balloons rolling over sewing pins.
Maybe that's what I should be doing. It would take a lot
to get my face in that position quite frankly.
Bowser's Castle in comparison is a piece of piss and
my hands –
where do they go? This is a nightmare. Oh he's just
stopped talking they're all looking at me. And what?

Lowri Llewelyn-Astley
(Highly Commended)

Melon

This week they start a unit on world geography. Miss Montgomery explains the morning's task: to create their own globe. There are several classroom assistants here because this is a Special School. Mr James is her favourite because he is very kind and patient when she doesn't understand and wears interesting ties.

He helps her blow up a balloon, and together they cover it in papier-mâché. Once dry, maybe tomorrow, they will carefully burst the balloon before painting their globe, mapping out entire continents, and Mr James will make sure Madagascar doesn't end up in North America.

Dolly's father is busy doing the washing as Dolly eats her after-school snack. Later he will help Dolly with her homework, before making her favourite dinner of Turkey Dinos, sketti and chips because today is Thursday. Afterwards he will load the dishwasher and let Dolly place the washing up tablet in the drawer and press 'On'. He will close his eyes as he dries her with the towel he heated on a radiator, and in front of the Discovery Channel he will comb her hair free of tangles as they drink cocoa.

This week they are studying Africa. Real Nigerian performers have come to visit wearing bright, extravagant costumes. Dolly plays one end of the *balofon*, a West African xylophone made of bamboo, with Mr James at the other. The head of the group, Oberhiri – Obi – wears deep scars on his cheeks.

'Did you have a scrap with a lion?' asks ADHD Dafydd, punching the air. 'Did you win?' No, Obi explains. This is a tribal custom called *scarification*. Family elders cut the little baby's face as a way of identifying their people. Much the same as herself, she thinks, with her flat facial features and upward slanting eyes.

After school, daddy makes Dolly a snack. He slices a watermelon, the biggest she has ever seen. She enjoys her snack; well – daddy promised her chocolate pudding later if she eats some fruit now – so she enjoys it as much as she can. She lets the juice drip down her chin, staining her shirt, to make sure daddy knows just how much she's enjoying it in case he considers revoking the pudding.

He stops ironing to watch her, bemused. 'You know you're supposed to spit the seeds out, don't you?'

'Oh. OK. They taste good,' says Dolly.

'Mrs Burke next door but one swallowed a seed and a melon grew in her belly. That's why she's so fat,' daddy winks.

Dolly finishes the rest of her melon, spitting out the seeds – she can't have a melon grow in her belly – she's too small for it to fit in there, and would surely explode.

This week they are studying South America. When the lunch bell rings, Mr James asks Dolly if she will stay behind and help him tidy up after a morning of Day of the Dead mask-making. He produces two lunch boxes from his bag. He knew he could count on her, he says. 'Burritos. Special Mexican food just for us.' He has something important to discuss with her, something Miss Montgomery doesn't want to teach the whole class yet.

'Do you know what 'sex' is, Dolly?' No, she says. Mr James explains the other pupils aren't ready; they won't understand. Dolly mustn't tell anyone what she's learned in case her classmates get jealous and angry; they scream and throw things enough as it is. Dolly is thrilled.

Sex is a special handshake, he explains. Grownups do it with other grownups they really like. Dolly is beside herself at being considered a grownup, more of a grownup than Muscular Dystrophy Martin and Severely Autistic Alice, Speech D-d-d-disorder Dean and ADHD Dafydd.

She understands. He tells her to meet him tomorrow lunchtime so he can show her how to do sex.

Miss Montgomery has taught them about all the continents, one by one. Handmade globes hang from the classroom roof like disco balls. Finally, they've made it to Australia, the final piece of the puzzle.

Dolly felt sick this morning. Daddy rinsed the vomit out of her hair, which tasted like last night's bangers and mash, making him late for work at the sausage factory. He wanted Dolly to have the day off, but she was adamant about Australia. She and daddy had recently watched a documentary on the Discovery Channel and she wanted Miss Montogmery to know she knew about the Aborigines, *indigenous* people of the continent who would go *walkabout* before they were hunted by Captain Cook and his people. There's a lot more to Australia than kangaroos, Dolly explained to Miss Montgomery.

This week her trousers have felt tighter than usual. She's been sneaking to the fridge when daddy is busy hoovering, or dusting the ornaments mummy forgot, and munching on slices of Edam cheese. When studying Europe, Miss Montgomery explained that Edam cheese is made in Holland, by people called the Dutch. Everybody rides bicycles there (probably so they don't get fat from all the cheese?). She has never much liked Edam, but lately she just can't get enough, even though it tastes like rubber. She will ask daddy to teach her how to ride a bike.

After school Dolly bounds up to her room, where she changes into looser clothing. Daddy shouts from downstairs, 'Would you like some fruit to keep you going until dinner, my little extra chromosome?' But even the thought of fruit makes her insides feel funny lately, even with the promise of chocolate for pudding. She takes the fruit so as not to hurt daddy's feelings and because she wants chocolate pudding, squashing the clementines and kiwis, apples and oranges, inside the doll house she hasn't played with since daddy bought her the dinosaur figures.

She stands stark naked in the mirror, looking the same as usual: short neck, flat nose and a tongue that seems to find its way out of her mouth before she's even noticed. Then she sees them, the red marks that streak her rounded belly. Suddenly, it hits her like a bunch of bananas. The watermelon. She turns every which way in the mirror in the hope it will disappear. It's already a fair-sized melon, not as big as the one she ate the day they made their globes, but still big.

She will tell daddy, she reasons. He'll know what to do. Yes; it will all be fine. It's frightening that she will have to explode, but she knows daddy struggles to pay for things with his job making sausages, which he only works while she is at school, like the dinosaurs she wanted after Mr James came to school wearing a dinosaur tie one day. At least once she has exploded he won't have to keep buying bigger shoes or haircuts and all the other things that never stay the same for long. But he will have a fresh watermelon to enjoy, all to himself, without having to share with Dolly.

Nicole Payan
(Commended)

Sweet Peas

It was the kind of country road that clichés were born on. The kind where imagining red barns and tractors came as naturally as breathing. It was also the type of road that had a deep and lasting friendship with the pickup trucks of decades past. Whether they were rusted out or well-maintained, typical red or muddy brown, it knew the multipurpose vehicles of the rural country well. It had shared many long seasons with the worn rubber of the wide tyres that had deepened its path over time. It may have been surprised, then, to find a very different kind of car was driving over its dusty stretch.

In contrast to the rough and tumble speed of the familiar trucks, the dainty crawl of this small, city car was utterly foreign under the blue of the country sky. So too was the glimmering silver paint job that was only slightly hidden by the skirt of dust it had gathered on its way. The driver positioned behind the windshield had a tight grip on the wheel. He squinted through his dark glasses, hoping that the tinted lenses would save him not only from the sun but also from the sight of his past home. He didn't want to be here.

Despite his reluctance to be anywhere close to his destination, Dan Hunter found himself reminiscing almost fondly as he passed familiar landmarks on the seemingly average road. He could pick out a few trees of the many that paraded past his left and label them as the ones he had climbed most often as a child. He knew which crooked fenceposts had been knocked out of alignment by his own doing. He recognized the minty green of the mailbox that signposted his mother's house before he could make out the numbers. This had been his home and it could have remained that way for his whole life. He would be the first, however, to admit that he no longer regarded the rundown dwelling he was creeping towards as his home, not anymore.

When he finally pulled off the road and came up the winding drive of the lot he could so easily recall, he couldn't make himself get out of the car. He sat in the safety of the air-conditioned interior as he stared at the wood siding and familiar front porch in front of him. The place had seen better days. Most of the white paint was almost entirely peeled off the front face of the house. At least three of the steps up to the porch were rotted out. And, although none of the windows were boarded up, they were so filthy there was no way to tell what they were hiding inside.

Dan considered turning back. After all, who would know? There wasn't another house for a quarter mile and Emily didn't have to know the truth. He sighed as he pulled off his sunglasses to rub at his eyes. His wife would know he wasn't being honest. She always knew.

With another deep sigh he pushed the door open and stepped into the afternoon sun. With his black sports jacket and shiny black shoes, he looked even less the country boy he had grown up as. He took the stairs carefully, only stepping in the edges of the risers. Dan tried the handle of the door before he started digging in his pockets for the key. It had been a surprise when the lawyers had given it to him; he hadn't known the house had locks in the first place. As expected, the door opened with just a twist to the handle.

Getting it to open produced a loud groan and a great stirring up of dust. He was reminded of how many years it had been since he had been there and why he so wanted to stay away. It didn't matter; he was here to satisfy Emily.

He tucked his hand into the inner pocket of his coat, feeling for the papers that would sell his inheritance. They didn't necessarily need the money, but it was of more use to him than an old home in the middle of nowhere. After all, it wasn't like he owed his mother anything. Hell, he hadn't spoken to her in ten years. She hadn't even called to tell him she was sick. He found out she was dead when the attorney called him to talk about her will. Why she had left him anything was beyond him. Surely she could have found someone else to give all her worldly possessions to. Someone who was part of her church family would have been more believable since he figured his mother had considered herself without a real family after he had left.

It was dark inside and flipping the switch by the door did nothing to change that. Dan scowled, then remembered that he hadn't paid for any utilities since he was handed the deed for this place. It was a good thing he hadn't taken this trip in the middle of winter. Everything was still in the house: furniture, keepsakes, a scrawled note by the door. Dan's eyes went to the pictures hanging in the front hall, the pictures of him and Chase. Although Chase was nearly two years older than Dan, they looked startlingly similar in their childhood photos. They had the same brown eyes, the same freckles, and the same dirty blonde hair that they both got from their mother. There were the pictures of them with friends, at fairs, at birthdays, and just running around outside. But, in all of them, the boys were together. People had always called them the Hunter twins.

The last picture of them standing together was at Chase's high school graduation. Dan ran a finger over the glass, clearing the dust to see his brother's wide smile as he held his diploma. That was the year that he decided he wanted to apply for scholarships and attend school in the city. He wanted to be an architect. With his mother firmly against it, however, Chase had been resigned to staying at home to keep her happy. The boys knew she was still hurting from their dad running out on them and Chase didn't want to give her anything else to be sad about. It was Dan who had convinced him to go. And it was Dan who had sat beside his weeping mother at the funeral, when Chase was killed in a hit and run, just four months after he moved out. As he continued through the house, he skipped the door on his immediate right, Chase's room. He remembered the feeling of emptiness that seeped out of the walls when he stood there all to well. He also passed by his room. There was nothing he wanted there that he hadn't taken when he had moved out. The back door that led to the porch was open and the only other thing that stood between him and the expanse of hip-deep grass and wild daisies was a cardboard box nearly full of bottles. When his mother had truly lost herself to drinking, Dan had given up trying to make her happy, trying to make her speak to him again and trying to get her to give up the alcoholic band-aid she seemed to think would help heal her pain.

A sparkle of green caught his gaze to the right and he turned to look into the kitchen. There was nothing there... and there was nothing here. He began to turn back towards the front door, but the green that had taunted him caught his attention again, this time on the squares of linoleum. It took him a moment to place the warped jade shape on the floor, but soon enough he brought his eyes to the windowsill, looking for the origin of the coloured light on the floor. Sure enough, there it was: his mother's green glass vase. The sun intensified as the small cloud that must have hidden it for moments moved on and the golden light caressed the soft curves of the humble vase, making it glow even through the dust and cobwebs that wreathed it, casting an evanescent twin on the floor.

Dan remembered it so well he could almost see it before him in a different time. When the kitchen cabinets were truly white and you could see the floral pattern on the linoleum floor without kicking at the dust. His mother would be wearing one of her aprons, her hair braided away from her smiling face. It would be late spring and the sun would be burning in a bright blue sky. Dan and Chase would run into the kitchen, their fists full of sweet peas, the first of the season. His mother had loved the smell of the tiny blossoms. Dan and Chase would buy her a few packages of seeds each year for her birthday and they never failed to plant them each fall. There hadn't been a summer without them until Chase had died. After that, Dan couldn't bring himself to walk into the store without his brother, let alone pick up a package of the almost sacred flowers. The vase had stood as empty as Chase's room for the first time since Dan could remember.

His footsteps towards the still barren vase left tracks in the dust. He missed the smell of the flowers and the smile of his mother. He reached out to brush the cobwebs away from the glass and caught sight of another strange object. He reached through the webs, grimacing in distaste as the frail nets clung to him with the stickiness of cotton candy. As he wiped his hand on his jeans, he took stock of what he had found. The sun had faded the writing on the small envelope, but its shape was completely familiar to him. He carefully opened the package and tipped it on its side. A few round seeds sprinkled out onto his open palm. Sweet-pea seeds.

He tipped his hand back to replace the seeds, trying to figure out what their presence could mean. As he watched his small handful trickle back into place, he noticed something else in the envelope, a thin slip of paper. He pulled it free.

Compared to the envelope, it was in good shape. Squinting slightly, he could still make out the lettering. He read his mother's cursive, her voice sounding in his head as he did so: 'For when he comes home.'

Dan didn't move for a long time, holding the seeds and the note in front of him as though they would save him from drowning in the wave of guilt and heartache that rushed over him.

Carefully laying both precious items on the counter, he pulled the buyer's papers from his pocket and stared at them for what seemed an even longer stretch of time. The setting sun began to fade in earnest and Dan could barely make out the writing on the forms he held. He shifted his gaze to the bare lattice out the window where the sweet peas should have been blooming.

The car that didn't belong drove into the blue hour of twilight and away. The home remained behind, as gloomy on the outside as it had been for many years. Inside, it was mostly the same as well — with the exception of a newly exposed hanger in the front hall where a picture had gone missing, a dust-free ring on the windowsill of the kitchen, and the addition of a heap of torn legal documents that iced the top of a collection of bottles by the back door.

Whyt Pugh

The Big Send Off

My complete lack of a corpse was rather inconvenient. This was my immediate problem: nobody I loved was dead, or even imminently dying. My parents are both very much alive and I don't have any siblings that could meet their demise under mysterious circumstances. I am completely lacking in terminally-ill grandparents; my mother's parents are happily (and unfortunately very vitally) living in Spain where I'm convinced their wrinkled skin is actually turning into leather and although I do have one dead grandmother, this death occurred some two decades ago and is therefore of no use to me in my current situation. My father's mother died when I was young enough not to remember and Bamps married a woman who truly believes she is ageing gracefully as Katharine Hepburn's long-lost twin sister. Well, whatever chemicals Glam Granny Beryl is injecting herself with, they appear to be working, for she stubbornly lingers on, a bit like Dracula really. I do have a few cousins going spare (car crash maybe?), but there is no way I could convince her that I am their next of kin. Besides, they're all kind of wankers, so let them rot in their hypothetical ditch.

Okay, now don't get the wrong impression – I'm not actually a psychopath who would orchestrate the death of a relative, however far removed. It would just be really, really handy to have a dead body right now. This leaves me with only one option: I am going to have to devise a deceased relation, create a carcass, craft a cadaver. Not literally, of course, I just need to convince her that I have a body that needs to be buried. This is the part I'm a bit nervous about, because I've never taken an acting class in my life. In fact, the closest I've ever come to thespianism was a certain DVD that my mate Ash smuggled to me in year nine and the title kinda rhymed with that, but yeah, nevermind. My first thought was to go to the swimming pool and float facedown for ages without any goggles on and think of what I was going to say, but the council closed the leisure centre. Cutbacks see, they must think fitness is overrated, let the NHS deal with that – it will come out of their budget then. Deciding austerity measures must be a laugh when you can drive your BMW to work-out on your private gym membership. Saltwater then, it is going to have to be saltwater.

The shop had been vacant for months, but then I noticed a change, the whole village noticed. First, it was painted a sage green, very vintage, quite attractive really. Thinking back on it, I remember seeing her do it herself, but in those white and formless overalls over which palette upon palette had wept, I did not notice her. I am ashamed of that now, of how intrinsically society has written my idea of beauty. Then came the sign, each wooden letter carefully cut out in a curved and inviting feminine script:

The Big Send Off

Where people had been whispering before, now they started to talk. Most people thought it was a travel agent, some a party supplies store, but then, when the shutters went up, a collective gasp swept from one end of the High Street to the other: it was a funeral director's.

How irreverent they said, how tacky. The curtain twitchers

and gossips said all sorts of things about her, but then two kids got killed on the new bypass and their parents took a chance on her and what she did changed what the town was talking about. It was beautiful they said – it wasn't really a funeral, it was a celebration. One young woman had been brave enough to ignore the idle rumours and because of that she had begun to dismantle the shell of grief that confined a shattered family. Naturally, I was curious and so, as inconspicuously as possible, I ordered a portion of chips to eat-in at the cafe across the street. My reconnaissance mission, however, gleaned me little information and it forced me to draw up a plan of observation. To avoid being a stalker (and to prevent impending cardiac arrest) I knew that I couldn't go to the café every day. I therefore had to calculate what days were likely to have the highest volume of deaths and, in the absence of statistics, decided on Tuesdays and Thursdays, as my uncle once told me that more planes fly over the valley on a Thursday than any other day. I know, I know, more people die in donkey-related accidents than plane crashes, but there are plenty of asses in Aberbranog.

By the time I was brave enough to enter the shop, I had eaten enough calories of starch to rename the café Stiffy's Chippy. I watched her rub the arms of women who smiled through their tears and squeeze the hands of taut-lipped men as her fingers lingered on theirs in recognition of what they did not say. She never wore the polyester Victorian mockery issued to those in the mortician's trade, just a felted green coat with asymmetrical buttons and brown boots over tight jeans. She was real and I was trying not to admit that I was mental.

I had pushed my time of watching over plausible limits and was forced to open my theatrical debut without any rehearsal. I rubbed the saltwater in my eyes before I came into view of the windows and bloody hell it hurt. Luckily, when I entered the shop she must've been in the back room and so I had a moment to breathe and let the weight of my fictitious grief anchor me to my resolve. The room was empty except for four large banners suspended on stands proportionally split in two. I walked to the advertisement on the far-left and began to decipher the message:

Going Green?
Make an *IMPACT* in the right way with our eco-inhumation service!
Leave the weeping to the Willows
with a made-to-measure
BASKET CASKET,
included <u>free</u>
when you select this package.

Um, okay. So does that mean you can recycle your relatives now? Maybe the next one would make more sense:

Voyage to Valhalla
Let your fallen warrior
sail into the afterlife
with this unique funeral plan.
Following the cremation,
your loved one's ashes
will grace the decks
of a scale model
wooden Viking ship.
Choose from a sea
or reservoir ceremony.
(Fire arrows and archer included).

I was actually quite intrigued by the idea and crossed the centre divide to the third poster:

Sleeping Beauty
Give your princess
the fairy-tale funeral
she deserves with our –

'Hello.'

I turned around swiftly, wide-eyed with shock and saline.

'I'm sorry that I didn't hear you come in. I was just putting the kettle on. Would you like a cup of tea?'

'Yes, please, that would be lovely.' Here I was, conversing with her quite normally. Her voice was measured, gentle. Of course it was – she daily navigated the newness of those robbed.

'Milk and sugar?'

'Just milk, thank you.'

'Please, have a seat in the consultation room.' She motioned to a doorway and I settled on a wicker two-seater with comfortable cushions. There was a canvas painting comprised of formless colours gazing down at me. It had no frame, as though to accommodate its expansion, as it swallowed my supposed sorrow. An emotion I could not name rose in me and was suppressed; my pulse had increased dramatically by the time she returned with the teas.

'My name is Sam Sutton and basically I'm here for whatever you need or want over the next few weeks.'

Damn, girl, I think that's a bit too generous on your part, let's get to know each other first…

'How are you feeling?'

'Numb. Afraid.' You lying bastard, playing the vulnerability card.

'Would you like to give me some details about the situation?'

'It's my grandmother, she died two days ago of a severe

stroke.' Well, that is kinda true.

'When it happens without warning, it can sometimes be the most difficult to process. What I would like you to do is to describe your grandmother for me – give me a picture of grandma as a person.'

'Well, she was one of those happy hosts. Her Welsh Cakes were the best in South Wales, let me tell you. She was a constant maker of sandwiches and teas, nobody went hungry. My grandmother always wore her housecoat for any task, regardless of the likelihood of the potential contaminant actually marring her clothing, but that is just how she was – a thorough woman, a woman of details. When my grandmother hugged you, her whole body and character hugged you – she was comfort epitomised.' You idiot, you just described the most stereotypical Welsh grandmother ever, not at all suspicious. Why didn't you add that she washed the front every Sunday and reminisced about blacking the grate, tin baths, and coal fires with astounding frequency?

'She sounds like a wonderful, caring woman. What's her name?'

Shit, I should have known this was coming. 'Um, Beryl.' Guess glam gran was good for something after all.

'Was she religious?'

'No, not at all.'

'Good.'

'Good?'

'It is just that the absence of religion will ease my plan. It is just preliminary at this point and feel free to jump in if you have any ideas. I think we should celebrate Beryl the way she celebrated those she loved – with food and lots of it. A tea party, in fact, with little sandwiches. I will source a most delightful array of cups, saucers, and tea-pots. Leave all the decorations to me and the baking, all I need you to do is see how many of those infamous housecoats you can round up. How does this sound so far?'

'Uh, good. Is this for after the service?'

'This *is* the service. I believe in commemorating the life of the person, not focusing on the death. I want to encapsulate your grandmother as a person in a fun and unique way to honour *her*, not an archetypal construct of mortality. I am a funeral planner, like a wedding planner, not a funeral director.'

'Well, yeah, that sounds tidy.'

'But, you are right – there should be a ceremony aspect. I was thinking that at the tea party we can make candles out of our cups and then we will gather around the grave at sunset for a tea light ceremony. But, not to end on a sombre note we will return to the venue for a Welsh Cake baking and housecoat decorating competition. Will she be buried or cremated?'

'Buried.' I didn't have any corpses to burn, or bury for that matter.

'Okay, has the doctor released the body yet?'

'No, they want to do a post-mortem.' Nice one butt, buying some time to procure a deceased volunteer to impersonate your wonderful, albeit non-existent, grandmother.

'That is very unusual as they know the cause of death.'

'She was down the pit so it is compulsory.' Stupid, stupid. Now, you've got a progressive pastry-making, pick-axe wielding granny undermining the institution from below ground.

'Well, well, your grandmother is getting more and more interesting. Would you like to incorporate mining into the ceremony?'

'Oh no, she didn't like to talk about what went on *down there*.'

'Not to worry, I have no intention of disclosing her

gynaecological records at the party.' She smiled.

Don't talk about female anatomy, you beautiful girl, I can't concentrate.

'If you don't mind, Ms. Sutton, I would rather that I be personally responsible for all the arrangements pertaining to the, um, body like. I will let you know when she is buried.' I am a master of deception, now all I needed to do was borrow a fresh, unmarked grave for about an hour. It is not like the occupant is going to mind, is it?

'If you are sure. You can always ask me for casket providers and things of that nature. Have you purchased a plot at the cem?'

'No, not yet.'

'I have a chart of all the available ones. Should we go there now and you can select the one that your grandmother would have loved?'

'Yes, that would be lovely, thank you.'

'Great. I will drive. Let me just go get my bag.'

When she had left, I began to think that I actually might be able to pull this off. I tried to ignore the fact that I had gotten in way over my head and a niggling feeling of that something I refused to name. I didn't want to consider that she would eventually find out and then who would want to date a psycho who hallucinates super-grannies?

She popped her head back in and my philosophical contemplation was cut short.

'Shall we go?'

'Yes.' I followed her to the road and got into the passenger side of the green Clio that she indicated.

It was a quiet journey to the cemetery. I remember watching her with the husbands, brothers, and fathers and recalled that this was her man approach: emotion is not masculine, men do not grieve.

'I forgot to ask, how much do you charge for your

service?'

'Nothing.'

'Nothing? Then how do you live?'

'Well, if a family has a large insurance pay-out then I accept some money from them and many families give me donations that add up. But, for the typical family, I feel that it would be morally bereft of me to add the stress of finding money at such a delicate time. Death is to be treated with compassion, not capitalised upon. As long as I take enough money in to pay the rent on the shop, then I can continue business.'

'That's good of you.'

'It is not about me. If I can show people how to begin to chip away at the immensity of the boulder weighing upon them that is grief, shock, guilt, and regret, then maybe someday they will be able to turn that stone to sculpture.'

This all made sense to me, but something struck me as a bit odd. We parked the car and began ascending the hill of proclamation where so many hands of stone rose tentatively into the air saying: I was here. I have always thought the grass in graveyards was a more vibrant shade of green than anywhere else, as though the roots suckled and transformed all the intentions cut short by fire and locked casket lid. Hey, if you get one of Sam's basket caskets you could actually *be* part of that grass. Maybe it is just the contrast created by the innumerable blades that persist despite frost and flood to the unmaking of bodies concealed beneath their vital cells. The late afternoon sun fell high on the quarry above, honey and slate from which all these people could have been carved. Even the heather stood starkly above us and cast a shadow too long for it to have possessed. As we climbed toward the vacancies at the back, Sam paused for a moment and asked if I would wait.

She made her way down the row of graves, carefully picking her way around each rise and fall as though her footsteps might disturb those beneath. Sam stopped at a small and indistinct marker, one that I would have overlooked had not the object of my infatuation turned her gaze upon it. From her pocket she extracted what looked like a glass pebble and placed it in a pot in front of the grave. She did not rise from her crouched position, but let her fingers taste each grain of stone. There was something so inexplicable, beyond tenderness or grief or love, in the mineral caress of her fingertips that I didn't realise until I was nearly there how I had been physically drawn toward the image of the stone woman.

I startled her with the clumsiness of the body that was too big for me and she shook the sediment of whatever I had witnessed from her as she rose quickly.

'I'm sorry,' she said walking away from the grave. 'Let's move on.'

She didn't want me to see the inscription torn from the rock that had survived glaciers, but I read as I followed her: *Seren Sutton.*

'At least you will get quite fit when you visit your grandmother, as all the available spaces are right at the top.' She was flustered, trying to draw the attention away from whatever had died inside her.

'Are you saying I am not fit already?'

'No comment.' She stopped. I stopped. 'How about one of these spaces?'

'This could work. I would like to get a feel for the position, see if Gran would have approved. Do you mind if we sit on this bench for a bit?'

'Of course not, I need to sit down after that walk anyway.'

The bench was cold and my already tense muscles contracted against it. It was also a rather small bench and I was very aware of how near my hand was to hers. The light had climbed higher into the crags and the grey of evening was moving over those mounds unmaking the molecules of the forgotten. I was drained of all I had ever been as I watched the coming darkness. Completely empty, I sat ashamed in the presence of someone who had spoken to death and turned back to life, volunteering to suture the irreconcilable. She was so much more of a person than I had thought possible, her pain was so perfectly polished. I didn't have those spaces within me to absorb any of her burden. All those things I couldn't see as I watched her from across the street I could see in the way her fingertips wrote her devotion in secret stone.

'What are the pebbles for?'

'Every time I help a family, I put one in the pot.'

'What will happen when the pot is full?'

'I will get a new pot.'

The light was slipping further away.

'Sam, I don't have a grandmother.'

'I know, but I still put a pebble in for you.'

'Would you like to go get some coffee?'

From the grey she turned her head and smiled softly at me.

'Yes, I'd like that.'

David Schönthal

Cairn

In the distance, where dark hillsides were softly merging into the dismal grey of a cloudy sky, small dyads of light were moving through the dusk in the early evening traffic. Some scattered trees could yet be made out as dark shadows against the remote hillsides, but the type of crop on the wide fields between the fireflies of the homebound cars and the brightly illuminated window was not recognisable any longer. It was late autumn. The sky was overcast with menacing rain clouds. Cold. Bleak. Cosy.

With his hands, Niklas was blocking out the bright light from his field of vision. He had his nose pressed against the cold windowpane and was inspecting his surroundings. Apart from the far-away hillsides, the trees, cars and vast fields, he could make out a small, fragile stone formation. Right in front of his window, where the fields ended abruptly in a small embankment, there was a cairn. Puzzled, Niklas inspected the construction, wondering what its purpose was. None at all? His eyes scrutinised the impressive artwork: the base was made of a block of stone of the size of a slightly oversized football. It was topped with further ever-smaller stones, balancing gingerly on one another, reaching a considerable height. Niklas guessed about three feet. On top of it all sat enthroned a tiny pebble, gloating. Niklas had to smile to himself when the formation reminded him of a vigilant meerkat on the lookout for danger. Someone must have put quite some time and effort into building this lonesome guardian. But why? And – for all the world – why here?

Niklas turned away from the window and looked at the book that was lying on the small table in front of him. *The Turn of the Screw* by Henry James. Up until just a few minutes ago, he had been reading in it, but had then got bored and put it away. Only then had he noticed that the train had stopped, and had started to observe the fall of dusk and the slow merging of colours into shades of grey outside his window. Now he once again picked up his reading and opened it on the page where he had left his bookmark. He took it out and placed it between two random pages somewhere earlier in the book. Then he resumed reading the chapter at the beginning of which he had started to drift off.

Not long after, he was again looking out the window, *The Turn of the Screw* resting on his lap. Today he was struggling to concentrate and stay focused. Niklas had had an arduous day at university. A day crammed with umpteen lectures and four hours of practical training in the chemistry lab. He was dead tired. The one-hour train ride didn't really do much to cheer him up either. It was in these moments when Niklas wondered why he bothered to commute to work every day and why he didn't just move to the city. He hated the suffocation of the overflowing wagons at rush hour. He couldn't stand the stentorian mobile conversations of his travelling companions. He didn't give a rat's arse about the love life of anonymous strangers, about the dinner that mummy had cooked and that would be waiting for them, or about the newest gossip and rumours of any old one-horse town. Today, he felt particularly entertained by a rough high-pitched voice a few compartments further down that was shouting her day's misery down the line. He loathed this petty small talk of other people's desperate attempt to kill time. At more quiet times he actually quite enjoyed a train ride. Usually he loved travelling, getting lost in a gripping novel, indulging in the magic of a different world, a different era. He thought of it as his own personal quality time. It was only at rush hour that he hated these hours of solitude, when the stuffy air was smothered in the palaver of his fellow passengers and the occasional mewl from a dissatisfied brat.

This time his eyes weren't wandering over the vast fields in the now almost murky evening. Instead, Niklas found himself mustering his fellow travellers in the mirror of his window. Opposite him sat a man in his forties. He was wearing a black suit. His grey coat and hat were hanging from a hook to his right, a big black umbrella propped up against the table. He too was absorbed in a book, his glasses deep down on his nose, concentrating. Niklas tried to make out the title of the book, but in the mirror he could only see its back cover and the man was covering the spine with his right hand. Next to Niklas, though not in his field of vision, was an elderly lady, her handbag on her lap. She had smiled at him timidly, when she asked whether the seat next to him was already taken. Now she seemed to be curiously inspecting the blue and green striped pattern on the empty seat opposite her. The other compartment was occupied by a family of four. The father was hiding his face in a big newspaper; the mother was staring forlornly out the window. Their offspring were sitting next to each other. The daughter was eagerly pushing buttons on a Game Boy, while her little brother was watching the screen in awe. Peacefully. From a few compartments further down, the high-pitched voice was recounting her latest shopping spree.

The train was still unmoving. Niklas returned his attention to his book. Having already forgotten their content, he was forced to reread the first three paragraphs of the current chapter.

A crack in the PA system.

'Ladies and gentlemen. Due to an accident involving people with a service travelling in the opposite direction, this train will be delayed by a further ten minutes. We apologise for any inconvenience caused and thank you for your understanding.'

The announcement was followed by a split second of deathly silence. Then the first sigh broke the spell and numerous passengers gave way to their irritation. A quiet 'Damn it! Not again!' was heard somewhere. People were shaking their heads. Niklas had looked up during the announcement, listening attentively, and was now focusing his glassy eyes on a spot in the air somewhere in the middle of the compartment. *An accident involving people* – is that what they called it nowadays? That's bonkers. Worst euphemism for suicide ever! – Accident involving people – ridiculous! He checked his watch. Ten to seven. Great! He was going to miss his connecting train. Another cheerful hour in a cold waiting room was awaiting him. This day was leaving much room for improvement still. He took out his phone and sent a text home. They would have to start dinner without him. Annoyed, Niklas returned to his novel and started reading the chapter anew.

'Hi mum!…just wan'ed to let you know that I'll be late. Some stupid twat jumped in front of a train and now I'm stuck here. I'll…I know, right?!…selfish bastard, he just… no, I'll be hungry still, leave me summing to heat up… yeah, there's…' Niklas forced himself to break away from the conversation. The phone bill of that dog's nightmare was probably being paid by someone else.

He looked out of his window again. Apart from the cars' headlights in the distance, the hillsides, trees, the cornfields and the clouds had dissolved into darkness. In the faint glow of the window, Niklas could just about still see a suggestion of the cairn. Other than that – nothing.

To pass the time, the elderly lady next to him had taken a tangerine out of her handbag, and was now peeling it delightedly. The fruity smell was hanging in the air and brought Niklas to turn away from the darkness outside. He looked around. The atmosphere in the wagon had, apart from a few impatient looks at the watch, returned to normality. The man in the black suit was still fully immersed in his book. During the announcement, he had briefly looked up, had rolled his eyes and had then returned to his read.

Followed by a few sighs of relief, the train jolted and was then set back in motion. Niklas started reading the chapter for the fourth time.

'Ladies and gentlemen, after an accident involving people at the next train station, we can now continue our journey with a delay of twenty-five minutes. Exceptionally, this train will halt at the next stop in order to pick up waiting passengers in our direction of travel. We apologise for any inconvenience caused and thank you for your understanding.'

Five minutes later, the train came in at the next station. Distracted by the sudden brightness outside, Niklas looked up from his book and absent-mindedly observed the scene passing slowly by his window. Three glittery golden specks on the opposite track all of a sudden yanked him back into reality. With a brief stutter, the train ground to a halt. Slightly to the left of his window, three blanket-sized coversheets were lying on the tracks, roughly four to five yards apart from one another. *At the train station?* The announcement – did they say *an accident at the next train station?!* – Niklas's head was racing. Under the three golden rags he could make out the form of a misshapen mass each. He didn't want to envision what it must have looked like underneath. Even so, his brain was torpedoed with images of beheaded torsos, separated extremities, loose heads with staring eyes wide open. A bloody hand, palm facing up, fingers curled, lying on the gravel.

The opposite platform was rammed with people, including police and emergency personnel, though most of the crowd was made up of spectators. Bystanders. No one seemed to be moving – or that's what it looked like to Niklas at least. The terrible reality of the three golden sheets between the train and the platform drew the full attention and, like a black hole, sucked up all sense and swallowed it, hungry for more. The audience. They were all wearing long grey coats, dark sunglasses, a grey hat. Even the police and emergency personnel were staring, their right hand propped on a big black umbrella, gloomily into the void. Indiscernibly, they merged into a grey wall of clothes. Then, there was nobody. Nothing. Nothing but the grey wall of the old train station and that unbearably blinding glitter on the tracks, reflecting the glare from the ceiling lights. Niklas blinked.

Half in trance, he heard the doors of the train shut, and felt a nudge against the small of his back as the train started to move again. He saw the large crowd shrink away behind him, bustling, shot a last glance at the mess on the tracks. Then, the scene had disappeared. For another while still, he saw the shadow of three dark specks dance a tango with the movement of his eyes, until his retina had recovered and they too vanished.

Niklas was ashamed. It had only been what – ten, maybe fifteen minutes ago? – that he was sitting on his seat, indifferent to the drama that was now behind him, but annoyed with the unfortunate circumstances. Annoyed that he would get home later than originally planned. That his dinner would get cold and he would have to eat alone. Thinking back, thinking back to a whole wagon vociferating their displeasure upon learning about *an accident involving people* through the loudspeakers, he felt nauseous. A high-pitched voice had let everybody know that she was worried about her dinner. A *twat* she had called him. *Him? Why him?!* And Niklas hadn't known any better either than to get angry over a two-hour delay. He was still angry in fact. Angry and ashamed. Damn it! – Twat!

Vigorously, he briefly shook his head and then looked away from the piece of air he had been staring at for so long. He hadn't noticed at all what had happened around him in the meantime. Now, he looked about. More people must have gotten on at the site of the accident now left behind. The corridor was jam-packed with people standing shoulder to shoulder. None of them wore a grey coat, nor did they wear sunglasses or grey hats. One man had a big black umbrella in his hand. The empty seat in Niklas' compartment was now occupied by a young woman. Her face was pale. Deadpan. Ghostlike. She was gazing into space. No smile, no frown, no nothing. Her mouth was slightly ajar. Paralysed into a silent 'Oh!' Other than that – nothing. Nothing. Apart from her eyes. Niklas faltered when he tried to focus on her eyes. Her stare was – Niklas had a hard time identifying the emotions behind her stare – her brown eyes, he felt, were drowning in fear.

Her posture was tense. With a stiff back, she clung to her bright green Wolfskin jacket, pressing it against her abdomen. Her bag was jammed between her feet.

'Are you not well, dear?' The tangerine lady to Niklas's right had bent forward and was looking amicably into the young woman's eyes. No one else took any note of her. The man opposite Niklas was calmly reading in his book, disinterested in the goings-on around him. The girl in the other compartment was now giving her brother instructions on how to win the next level on their Game

Boy. The high-pitched voice was yet again gossiping down her phone. The young woman didn't react to the friendly inquiry of her opposite.

Niklas didn't know why, years later, he would still remember the shock in that young woman's face. He would also never be able to explain to himself why he could still remember that ridiculous stone guardian outside his train window. A guardian that, by now, had probably been tumbled over by wind and weather. By time. A heap of rocks. An illusion he wouldn't even be certain anymore it ever existed. And the smell of a newly peeled tangerine.

Niklas grabbed his book and started reading the chapter anew.

Luke Smith

No More Bets Please

Check the jackpots. That's the first thing Jake does, after we stamp out our fags on the doorstep and wade into Coral, William Hill or, as it just so happens today, Laddies. He scuttles into the room sideways like a crab, rubbing his hands together, gazing up at the television screens, as if he was checking out the 3:15 at Wolverhampton. Jake nodded at the other punters, but no one looked up from their stools. Progressing towards the fab four at the back of the store, Jake jabs his chubby index finger into the grubby touchscreens before quickly retracting it from each, as though the screens let off a sharp convulsive shock.

My routine's a little more dignified. I walk towards the counter, head down, counting the notes in my wallet. Slowly raising my head, I aim my most insolent toothy grin towards the two cashiers in their sunburnt uniforms. Today I'm pretty loaded, so I pull out my wad, fan myself with it, and watch on as the cashiers' pupils follow its journey across my face.

'Month's wage for you here fellas. Well, that is if you split it between the two of you.'

'Luffs in, iz it Lee?' Mike asked. He has this speech impediment. When he speaks, he balances his pound coin-coloured upper teeth upon his lower lip, as though he's speaking into a fan on full power.

'What?'

'I said, Luff's in iz it?'

'He said, 'Your luck's in, is it Lee?'' the new guy repeated.

'Nah, born lucky fellas. What I've got is skill, a superfluous attribute for working here.' I wasn't sure if superfluous was the right word, but they weren't about to call me on it, not here, and certainly not in those uniforms.

Catching my eye across the room, Jake nodded towards terminal three. 'So, if you'll excuse me, gentlemen, I have business to attend to.'

'Lucky number three is it?' I asked, parking myself on the stool in front of number four. Jake dropped all his JSA playing Tutti-Frutti on number three last week. He's careless like that.

Having already fed a couple of pounds in, he proceeded to feed a few more in and opted for a super spin, but was spun super dry instead. Three lemons winked back at Jake; the last slot continued to spin before revealing a rotten plum that looked rather pleased with itself. A leprechaun's pot of gold illustrated the jackpot, and it was growing by the bet at the expense of Jake's funds, which ebbed beneath the flashing collect graphic. Jake pulled a creased tenner out of his jeans, and ironed it out with his palm against the side of the machine.

I looked away. Mug's game. I know it, the cashiers know it, and just about every punter in the joint knows it, but nobody told Jake. No wait, fuck that, everybody had, but you know what Gekko says about a fool and his money: 'It's a miracle they get together in the first place.'

I tapped the screen for the roulette. Why? Maybe because you know where you are with red or black, maybe because there's something reassuring about the colour of the virtual green mat, the colour of real American money. Or maybe because the house has only a 2.7% built-in advantage, as opposed to the 6% advantage it has over the slot games, which allows a guy like me to even the playing field out through his skill.

I like to start with a nice random spread of about twenty-five numbers across the mat with stakes between twenty-five and fifty pence. Trust me, it's best to keep it light around the tenner mark to start with. Slapping the flashing red bet button, I looked up at the T.V. hanging above me. Wimbledon was on, and some blonde bird with an unpronounceable surname was playing Serena Williams. Serena hadn't lost a match all year, but was in a bit of difficulty here, serving to keep in the set. I had a nice multiplier going on, and was up about seven quid so I hit the repeat button. No need to reinvent the wheel just yet.

'How about some in play action on Serena, if she loses this set?' I asked, swivelling my chair to face Jake; the jackpot had reached its half tonne maximum, and he had lowered his stakes to twenty five pence in response to his dwindling bank.

'How much?'

'Thirty should do.'

'Who's she playing?' Jake asked, his head spinning from the machine to the television. Jake has this habit of pacing back and forth from the machine, and averting his eyes from the screen when the spin comes in, as if looking at the screen was like getting caught leering at a young girl's chest.

There is nothing I hate more than superstitious gamblers. Some of these losers have to play on the same machine every time, as if one's luckier than the other. They kick off at you if you're up so much as a pound on 'their machine,' blaming you because they've pissed away their monthly mortgage repayment or the tuition for Junior's hospitality diploma on a neighbouring, identically-programmed machine. That's how these degenerates start with superstitions like Jake's.

'Lisitzkey or something,' I said, spinning back to my

screen, as my balance rose by four quid.

'Lisicki? She got to the semis in 2011.'

'Yeah, but Serena's gonna win it this year.'

Jake nodded in agreement: 'Put thirty on if it's 9/1, but pop twenty on if it's 12/1.'

'9/1 is too good a price to turn down on Serena Williams.' The Bet in Play radio presenter's voice filtered through the room in that assured estuary accent that you only ever hear on TV.

Hovering in front of me in the queue, Tudor was going through his usual obsessive compulsive routine, repeating the odds no less than five times to the new cashier before eventually counting out the fifty pence stake he had riding on Wolverhampton, in coppers of course.

'I've gotta go now Mike, mine's in play,' I said, elbowing past the only woman in the joint, who was clutching a forest worth of Irish lottery tickets.

'Al's gotta suff you. He hasn't done a Bet in Play yet.' Mike's chapped lips twitched upwards, as he suppressed a grin.

'You know you look like you're having a stroke or something when you do that Mike? Fine', I said, shooting the new guy a toothy grin, 'leave it to the punter to teach the staff how to do their fucking job here.'

Examining my slip, the new guy returned an especially false grin: 'Still locked in at 9/1. Pretty conservative price if you ask me. Williams has forgotten what it's like to be behind.'

'Laddies don't pay you to think.'

'No, I just take the money. That a three or an eight?' He pointed to my stake.

'What do you think? Am I gonna have to teach you to count too? Jake's is a thirty and mine's an eighty.' They were both thirties, but fuck him. So I make eight hundred instead of three. My wallet may have been lighter, but it was only temporary.

'It's your handwriting that's the problem, not my maths,' he replied, slamming my receipts on the counter.

'Then learn to fucking read.'

'Surely he's unemployable,' I said to Jake, who had moved from Tutti-Frutti to Deal or no Deal and was faring no better.

'Who, me?'

'Forget it.'

'Lend me some cash till my money comes in on Thursday?'

'Can't,' I said, pulling a still impressive wad from my wallet, feeding my receipt back into the machine and fingering an even spread across the roulette table. 'Besides, what do we pay your dole for? You should be budgeting.'

'Come on, you're fucking loaded, and you nicked that from your Nan anyway.'

'Fuck off you scrounger. I didn't nick shit. I'll get it back to her anyway.' Cheeky prick. I ought to have clipped him. His begging had already cost me three bets in a row, and now I was down to my original cash.

'Alright, whatever...look,' he said leaning conspiringly over my shoulder, 'Williams is four-one up in the second. I'll give you your money back from the winnings.'

Now then, you guys with the team might call Jake an enabler, but I see him for what he really is, a parasitic disabler eating away at my capacity to bet.

'Fine, here's twenty.'

'Is that all? Come on, my stake alone on Williams is thirty. Give us that at least.'

'Parasite.' I handed over another tenner, and he snatched it with a contemptuous shake of his head.

'So tight'.

'Whatever, I want that back as soon as we collect.'

Serena had just won the second set, and looked set to net me a cool eight hundred. So much for the new boy's 'conservative price.' That's why he's behind the counter, and I'm in front of it. He's paid to serve, whilst I'm paid to think. Some pretty good tennis analogies there. I wish I had thought of them at the time.

I returned to the roulette and reset my chips, but my spreads were too big. The ball refused to land on a high roller. I couldn't focus; I was making about thirty pence one bet, and losing three pound on another. I tried to ignore the tennis but, as I'm sure you can imagine, it's pretty tough to keep your mind on your money when you're twenty minutes from some serious cash.

You know how last session the nurse mentioned endorphins. Well I guess my body must have been secreting a couple of thousand endorphins with every serve. It's almost as if I already had the winnings in my wallet, and I stress *almost*, because the *almost* is the exciting bit. The *almost* is the feeling that you've got some inside information on the future, and you know how it's all going to end. You're going to end a winner. That's the high, *almost*. I was already spending the winnings: I would repay Nan, or get her an expensive gift. For myself? One hell of a weekender with Jake, who would have won a modest three hundred himself. I would let him off the thirty he owes me – after all, what are friends for?

'Shit,' she's bottled it,' Jake was laughing. Skint again, he stood with his arms folded in front of the T.V.

'Lisicki?'

'No, Serena. She's serving to stay in this, who could have seen that coming?'

He was right too, who could have seen that coming? By the looks of things not even Lisicki saw it coming, but it was happening, and Serena didn't seem to care, at least not like me. She didn't even hold serve.

Jake whistled. 'Game, set and match. Told you Lisicki was good. I'm down like seventy now.'

'You owe me thirty too.'

'Gotta pay my uncle first.... Pub?'

'I'll have to catch up.'

'Alright mate. You know it sort of feels like I've lost three hundred of my own money, funny that innit?'

'Yeah, that is funny,' I said. Goddamned parasite.

At that point, I had lost about one hundred and twenty. In Tuesday's session with Dr Ambrose, I said that it wasn't what I had lost that hurt, but what I had failed to gain. Dr Ambrose reckoned that was a sign of progress, but I thought that that was pretty obvious from the start.

Jake screwing me out of thirty quid was no big deal, and technically I had only lost eighty, but I knew that I *almost* had eight hundred. That made me nauseous. That's when the buzzing began in my ears, quiet like an air conditioning vent at first, but then it pierced through the ear like a syringe full of warm water. I smelt burning hair, then I tasted it too, and I couldn't swallow. Shouting for the desk to buzz the cubicle open, I clutched my twisting stomach and headed for the toilet.

The smell of burning hair was stronger now, but I no longer needed to go. My breathing settled, and my head began to clear as I cooled my burning cheeks in the basin.

Under the flickering, energy-saving bulbs, I stared at my translucent reflection, wanted to cry but didn't. It really isn't that bad, I told myself. So I had been on a poor run on the roulette, and got burnt on some in play, but that'll change. It's a matter of probability. The only question was whether I was willing to take advantage of it.

Here's where your crisis team's short story idea hits a bit of a snag. Firstly, I've never even read a short story. Back at school, we read *Of Mice and Men*, and that was kind of short, but I never even read that. It was a school copy and someone had written on the very first page that George kills Lennie because Lennie killed Curly's girl. Sorry for the spoiler, if you hadn't read it either. I ought to thank the guy really; he saved me a few hours. Honestly, is there any point in reading something when we already know how it ends? You already know more about the ending to this than I care to know. Anyway, how am I supposed to describe events that I can't even remember? Am I supposed to believe what some lying prick like Mike says? Or do I, as Dr Ambrose suggests, attempt to recount it through my emotional senses? I'll try both.

So I had been grinding my teeth like chewing gum all day, and the entire left side of my skull was throbbing like an open sore when I retook my seat. I needed a strong start on the machines to ease the tension. So I made bigger, more concentrated bets on the roulette, betting only on central red numbers. As I prodded the screen, the speakers emitted a popping sound that resonated through my ears, but I held my finger steady like the virtual hostess's voice. She took my twenty quid balance into the interface, as the ball tumbled towards thirteen black. I was born on July thirteenth and usually place about three quid's worth on thirteen black. But that was okay. It had to land on a red next. I fed another twenty into the machine, and hit repeat.

'No more bets, please,' the machine said, and seconds later the virtual ball spun around the wheel, and came to rest on black seventeen. Another twenty down, and another twenty seconds to make a decision, but logic prevailed once again. I fed my remaining fifty into the machine. I slapped repeat with a numb, sweaty hand, and that's when the ball acts against all logic and sense by choosing thirty three black.

What could I do? I couldn't switch to black now, because red was next. So I hit repeat.

I can still hear those words drawn-out like an elastic band ready to fly: 'No. More. Bets. Please'. My pupils spun with the ball, as it raced and then stalled across the wheel before returning to thirteen black. I couldn't move from the nausea, but I wouldn't have moved if I could. The next one will be red. All I have to do is hit repeat, and then collect my winnings.

Yesterday, you asked me what I now think of fixed odds betting machines. I couldn't answer. You told me to think about it and include it in this short story. You told me that they have been dubbed the crack cocaine of gambling. I'm not surprised, but you and I know better than to think it's that simple. I may not know much about crack, but I am willing to bet that crack addicts can still follow the football without worrying about the commercials or being consumed by the sense that you can *almost* see how it's all going to end.

I must have gone back up to the counter, head down, counting the receipts in my wallet, as I pulled her credit card out. 'Terminal four, just save the digits, and add more when I say.' I didn't look at Mike.

Returning to my seat, I jabbed repeat: 'No more bets please.' Red will come in. I will end a winner. And the end is *almost* here; it's coming in, it's now, right about now, any second now.

Daniel Williams

Thinking in English

Ask; you commit the acoustics
of each phrase to the air and wait.
Visibly, he receives your slip
in syntax, returns it
re-ordered and indicates,
finally, '*That way.*'

You follow the line of his gesture
to where its guidance ends
at the next corner;
you thank him, leaning
on your borrowed voice, unstable
in foreign weather.

You are native, somewhere;
you have felt, even there, how the pauses
splitting one word from another
can lengthen like crossing
from border
to border;

how the most familiar is often found
unfixed, and stalled speech gives

to proto-language,
where a palm outstretched
means *love*
or *hunger*.

Taking Place

From a series of photographs depicting paired buildings; one occupied, one abandoned.

(i)

Symmetry ends
at the seam they share
like border country.

A fracture in the would-be living room's hollow
window is the first sign of harm:
the immobile door, grown arthritic with waiting,

aches on its hinges. Up one storey
to the vacated bedroom, water reclaiming
its high corners, and the floor debris-strewn

with what they could not carry:
the bed, the mirror's outlook, still as relics under
exhibition glass.

(ii)

Through the dividing wall, heat presses
as a kitchen is set to purpose; the TV jangles
its transmission on schedule,

until the lit rooms are struck out
one by one;
routines are kept

to assure us we are not so far
adrift. Poised on the doorstep's precipice,
feel along the key's edge, its indents

betraying a guarded
claim to a lock, and the life
assembled behind it.

Taking Place responds to an image which can be found here:
www.camilojosevergara.com/Camden/Paired-Houses/5.

Jessica Winterton

The Oozlum Bird

I were cruising up the A65 in my new Land Rover. It drove like a dream. Got it off a guy I used to work with who bought it brand new then decided to emigrate. Needed to get rid pretty quick. Twelve grand, thirty thousand on the clock, MOT'd, Santorini Black Metallic, premium leather interior, automatic – done. Hey, I'm a Yorkshireman, I can appreciate a bargain!

Had me at 'Mate, I need to get rid of Land Rover' to be right, though. Wanted one since I were yay high and we went together like a wink and a smile.

We – I were trying to think of a name for her; cars have to be *hers*, don't they? – were on the last leg of our impromptu road trip, having worked our way up through the Peak District. Stopped occasionally to wolf something down and take some shots of the heathery valleys, cut up with dry stone walls. Fresh air, birds singing, no signal – perfect. All being well we were on track to see the sun go down on Lake Windermere. I probably wouldn't make it much past that, though. Especially not if the B&B I'd booked for a steal on Laterooms were half as comfy as it looked. I were cream crackered to say the least.

I decided to christen the radio. It had a good rummage in the ether and pulled up Radio 4. A woman's voice – some academic – were wittering on: '...so, yes it is possible that the decrease in divorce figures could be attributed to economic decline –' I turned it off.

'Chuff that for a game of soldiers,' I said to myself. Sod's law, just as I'd nearly forgot –

I got distracted by flashing lights behind me. Not blue like a police car or an ambulance, but headlights. Flashing headlights from the car behind reflecting in the rear view. It were a woman in the driving seat. Past that I couldn't tell, except that she were on her own in the little green Corsa. Then she starts beeping, driving right up my arse.

'I'm going at forty, love,' I said – like I were expecting her to hear me? – and I looked out in front. The road were straight as a die for near on three miles. Nothing on it. 'Just go round if you're that bothered!' I shouted when she kept on beeping. But I held my ground. There's usually a speed sniper somewhere on that road, as if I were going to risk it in a brand new car? Well, brand new to me. But still, she were flashing and beeping and waving and nearly bumper to bumper at the back end. It were an accident waiting to happen; and it were starting to get right up my nose. I recce'd along the side of the road. There were nowhere for a police car to hide on that stretch of it, not a speed camera in sight. So, I hit the accelerator and put some distance between me and her. I broke on the skid onto the tiny grass verge before she had chance to catch up. She careered past me, still bloody beeping. 'Daft cow,' I said, under my breath.

I sat a second trying to calm down. Then my phone started buzzing on the passenger seat. So much for no signal. I tried to ignore it. I couldn't. So I threw it in the glove compartment and slammed it shut, out of sight but not out of mind. I could still hear it grinding against the plastic on the inside. I gave up on calming down.

I were just about to fire the engine up again when I

realised the little green Corsa had u-turned and were pulling up on to the grass verge, facing me. There were thick, plastic eyelashes stuck around the top of each headlight. P plate stuck beside the M reg licence plate. Here we go, I thought.

She got out of the car and trotted over to my Land Rover, dodging puddles in the waterlogged grass even though she were well kitted-out in some serious-looking walking boots. She were looking a damned sight more windswept when she knocked on my window than she had when she got out of her Corsa. I realised just how much I were protected from the elements inside my Land Rover. I wound the window down and felt them – full blast in the face – for myself.

'There's something on top of your car,' she said, before I could get a word in edgeways.

'Sorry?'

'Something on top of your car,' she said again, slowing it down in what I were pretty sure were a Manchester accent. 'It looks like it's stuck on your aerial.'

'What kind of a something?'

'Looks like a camera bag.' She shifted out of the way as I opened the door and launched myself up off the step. Camera bag, seriously? As if I were daft enough to leave my –

My camera were on top of my car. 'That's why I was beeping at you. I figured a kit that big had to be a bit on the expensive side.'

'Two and a half grand,' I said, eyes glued to the canvas bag: visions of Canon crushed under Michelin treads. Oh, it went straight through me. It didn't bear thinking about.

'*Two and a half grand*?' I heard her cry – that's the only word for it –from behind me.

'Not including lenses.' They were in there as well. She um'd and ah'd for a bit before settling on: 'Wow.'

I must have put it on the roof as I got back in at the last pit stop. Forgot all about it. There were the lightest scratch across the paintwork that ran from front to back where the zip must have caught. The strap had wrapped itself round the flimsy aerial. How it hadn't fallen off only God knew.

I went round the back and retrieved it like I were handling a new born, placed it dead careful on the back seat. 'Is it ok?' she asked. She sounded concerned.

Every word in the English language exited the building there and then. I were too busy preparing myself for the worst. I couldn't afford a new camera, not now I'd blown near every penny of my savings on my Land Rover and I were pretty sure my insurance didn't cover my own stupidity.

'Thanks for...letting me know,' I said, in the end. She were standing there like a lemon, bless her, getting more weather-beaten by the second. I took back calling her a daft cow.

'You're welcome.'

'I mean really, really, thank you.'

'It's ok,' she said, pulling her hands into the sleeves of a jumper that practically drowned her and pushing her hair out of her face. 'It'll be alright.' She were really sympathetic. 'They're more padding than bag them things.' And she smiled. 'Safe travels.'

'You too.' Then she turned back towards her Corsa.

She took her time getting off. I could hear her opening and closing doors and out of the corner of my eye saw her faffing with something on the passenger seat. I tried not to look. Tried to concentrate on getting my camera bag open and surveying the damage. But, honestly, I didn't want to know. Not until I could have my brewing nervous breakdown in peace.

My phone were still drilling like a woodpecker against the inside of the glove compartment. It stopped just long enough for a redial and then off it went again. I leaned against my Land Rover and looked inland over the windy Dales. All grassy hills and grazing sheep. The sun were falling into its red band above a horizon that were mostly trees. Picture perfect.

'Twist the knife, why don't you?'

I heard a door slam on the little green Corsa, driver's side. She were putting her seat belt on. I gave her a wave, mouthed 'Thank you.' She gave me an okay sign back through the windscreen and then off she drove. I watched the Corsa shrink for a while. Put off the inevitable before turning back to my camera bag. But I couldn't psyche myself up for it. I had too many thoughts trying to play Tetris in my brain and getting stacked up all wrong.

And all I could hear were that incessant bastard phone!

I shouldn't've left it. It might've been Adrian with work for me for after I got back. But then what if it were Adrian with work for me for after I got back? Then I'd have to tell him that my camera were FUBAR and he'd want to know why but I couldn't tell him because he'd know it weren't like me to do something so daft and then he'd start picking because that's what he's like, picking and picking and picking until I lost my rag because I didn't – want to – talk about it!

I couldn't take the noise any more. I didn't care who were on the other end, the bugger were getting turned off.

I jumped back in the driver's seat and flung open the glove compartment with so much force that the phone literally jumped out. On instinct, I tried to catch it but it were like trying to catch a bar of soap in the bath. I finished up head first in the passenger footwell with my legs tangled round the steering wheel.

Lots of bumbling about and swearing later – you try getting up from there, I tell you, it's a nightmare – I finally managed to get myself right side up. But where the hell had my phone disappeared to? Well, at least it weren't ringing anymore.

'Connor?' I jumped and my heart landed in my mouth. '*Connor*?' The voice were cracklingly loud and coming from under the passenger seat. 'Connor Morgan don't you dare ignore me, I've had enough of that! Say something for God's sake!'

'Oh shit,' I said, before I realised I'd said it.

'Could you manage something a bit less inflammatory, do you think? Maybe 'Hi Dad, sorry I've not picked up the phone all month'?'

'Jack, there doesn't need to be –' said another crackly voice that I couldn't hardly hear. But I could hear she sounded upset.

'Yes, there does 'need to be.' We've been worried half daft!' I let out a hard blow and steeled myself for the unavoidable. Trying not to stage a repeat of the head in the footwell incident, I lay flat against the seats and reached blind under the passenger side while Mum and Dad muttered it out between them.

'Jack, he's just upset –'

'It weren't his problem to get upset about –'

'It's not going to help if you –'

'He can't just go disappearing like that –'

'He's a grown man –'

'Should have learned to stop just thinking about himself then.' Eventually, I put my hand on it. Call in progress, on speakerphone.

'I can hear you, you know,' I said, holding the phone up to my mouth.

'Good,' said Dad, 'I'm putting you on to your mum, she's been in bits.'

'Dad, I can't talk now –'

'Hello?' she said, croaky-voiced and snuffly. The digital clock on the dash crawled through three whole minutes before I managed the lamest 'Hi Mum.'

'How are you?'

'Plodding on.' Awkward. It took another long, long

silence for one of us to get to the point. I inwardly blamed hereditary Britishness for that old chestnut.

'Luke and Sarah said they'd talked to you.'

'Yeah.'

'Look, I don't want to talk like this over the phone, love,' she said. 'Can't we come over? Or you come to us? Whichever's better for you.'

'I'm...I'm not at home at the moment.'

'You working away again?' Her voice perked up a bit. She's always interested in what work throws up for me, where it takes me.

'Er, sort of. I don't know what you'd want me to say,' I admitted. And I didn't, I really didn't.

'We just need to get to the bottom of this.'

'Mum, the bottom of this is you had an affair.'

'Connor, I'm not making excuses –'

'Good.'

'But your dad has been the bigger man.'

'He's been a mug if you ask me!' I were fizzing. I'd had a month to stew over it with my brother and sister occasionally checking in to bend my ear. It were alright now, Mum and Dad weren't splitting up any more. Couldn't we just forget all about it?

I'd used up a lot of energy on envy that month. Luke and Sarah were Dad all over. The power of genetics gave them the ability to make like the Oozlum bird and disappear up their own arses without a moment's notice and feel all the better for it. Me on the other hand, I were all Mum. I got everything from the curly brown hair to the death-warmed-up complexion, the brown eyes, the creativity, the borderline self-destructiveness that meant this were set to be my first holiday for three years. What if genetics had something else tucked up its sleeve?

I worked away most of the time. I stayed in a lot of hotels.

I usually – in the absence of buying Land Rovers – had some money tucked away somewhere. I'd never needed to point it out yet to any woman I'd even come close to dating that I had means and opportunity in spades. But what if a genetic leaning towards motive were waiting in the wings for me? The argument – the stonewall belief – that straying weren't in my nature any more than it were my mum's...it didn't wash anymore, did it?

There's nothing worse than making your mum cry. Even when you're angry, there is nothing worse than making your mum cry. 'I didn't mean that, Mum. Dad's not a mug. I'm sorry.'

'So, that's what's got her so upset, is it?' It were Dad. Shit.

'I'm sorry, Dad. I didn't –'

'I'm going to try and sort your mum out,' he said. Then the line went dead. I tried ringing back. Over and over again I listened to it ring out. Karma, come back to bite me.

I stared out the windscreen. I'd missed the sunset on Lake Windermere. Now the darkness kept me blind outside the LED-lit interior of my Land Rover. Probably cutting my check-in a bit fine too. I sent a text to the mobile number I'd been given as a contact for the B&B, saying I were running late. I didn't want to go back out on the road again for a bit just in case Mum or Dad rang back and I couldn't pull over. Then again, I could be waiting there all month.

I paid enough attention to the headlights coming up the road towards me to flip the hazards on. Being so dark I didn't want to give Karma another chance to have a pop at me. Then they started slowing down. They stopped in the empty road, level with my Land Rover. I had to turn my headlights on to get a decent look at what turned out to be the little green Corsa.

She wound the window down. I followed suit.

'You still here?' she said, with a big smile on her face.

'Fraid so.'

'How's the camera?' I shrugged.

'I haven't looked yet.'

'Ah, the old Oozlum bird trick, eh?' I must have blank stared her for longer than I thought. 'It was a joke.'

'No, I know, sorry I, er...' and I started laughing. Borderline hysterical laughing. I thought she'd be looking at me like I'd got three heads but then I heard her laughing as well.

'Sorry,' I said, 'it's been a long day.'

'Aren't they all?' she said back, still smiling. 'You broke down now as well? Need a jump start?'

'No, no, I'm fine,' I managed, the cogs still going round.

'You sure?'

'Yeah. Thanks.'

'Alright.' And she set me with eyes black as the ace of spades. She said, 'Take care of yourself,' and really seemed to mean it.

'Thanks, you too.' I gave her a smile. Thinking about it, she actually seemed like a really nice girl. It crossed my mind that maybe I'd like to see her again. But on a dark road in the middle of nowhere? You just don't, do you? Then the road were empty again. The Corsa miles behind me. But it's alright, I thought, grinning like a Cheshire cat. I'm an Oozlum bird.

Liz Wride
(Commended)

Welsh Dragons

It all started on St David's Day.

Every March the first, we'd jump on the bus, as it slowly climbed the mountain to my Gran's house. Every March the first, my Dad would curse the Welsh landscape. 'Carn buleeve 'ey bludee stuck 'em alla wayup 'ere. Outta sight, outta mind. An' it'll bugger the bus's suspension right up, wun it?' Every March the first, my Mam would wonder why she could never get her daffs to be as bight and as buttery yellow as the ones that lined the lawn outside Gran's house. 'Blud an' bone, innit?' my Dad said quietly, thinking we couldn't hear. 'Blud an' bludee bone... blood an' bludee bone.'

*

They always decked my Gran's house out for the occasion: Welsh dragons on bunting, daffodils stuck on the doors of the bingo room... and a receptionist who couldn't respond to 'Bore Da.' We'd walk the corridor to her room, smelling that musty smell, old-people smell. My Dad said that was what knowledge smelled like after it'd been in your brain for years and years... so I made a conscious decision to stop trying so hard in school.

My Dad would be the first in through the door, always. 'Just in case, innit?' he'd say to my Mam, when he thought we weren't listening. There sat my Gran, her hair like pale candy floss, her skin the same shade as the china she was drinking tea out of. The only colour came from the glowing embers of her cigarette. It seemed to dwindle between her fingers, before reappearing in an instant: fully-formed and yet-to-be-lit. Once, I asked her why she smoked, and she said she needed it to warm the cockles of her heart and keep the fire lit in her belly. My Mam told me I couldn't light the fire in my belly until I was sixteen; even then, she'd make sure the shopkeeper didn't sell me anything.

Every year, Gran would give us presents to mark the occasion: bunch of daffodils (probably uprooted from the front garden), leek soup, clip round the ear.... But that year, when I was thirteen, she gave me a bloody big, huge, massive, egg. For once, my brother actually looked grateful for his tin of soup.

'Ta, Gran...' I mumbled. *What was I supposed to do? Crack it open and go for a World-Record-Attempt-Omelette? Paint it, and wait for Easter?* She just leaned in, and I got a wiff of that cloudy, smoky, lavender smell, again.

'Keep it warm,' she said. Of course, she gave the same instructions to my brother about the leek soup.

Then, as had become customary, as my Gran had done since me and my brother were little, she took us to the window, and pointed to the mountain. At the age of fourteen, I'd heard the story so many times, I could recite the words as she spoke them. 'A dragon lives up there, yew know...' she said. 'And that dragon...she is the mountain, yew know. It was down to her that we had that great, big, huge, mining disaster when I was a girl. They all said it were her, the dragon. All blamed her. But she hadn't done nothing. All she'd done were flap her wings as she woke up from her hibernation. She'd given a roar or two. She breathed a little fire. The mine caved in, there were explosions...all because

133

she decided to wake up.' My Gran would always pause at the end of the story, for dramatic effect. 'Now, mind…if anyone tries to tell you that it was just the faulty workings of the mine, or some kids setting the bracken alight, you tell them, it were the dragon.'

After the story, we always shuffled into the bingo room to watch the rugby. That year, the old Welsh man who rooted for the English was absent. My Gran told us: 'He'd gone the same way as all those uthur vegetables, he had…Alright one day…couldn't even feed himself the next…' before adding slyly, 'if I ever get like that…pull the plug, mun.'

In that moment, in my head, my Gran had more power than the National Grid. She seemed to simultaneously run on fossil fuels and electricity. In that moment, in my head, my Gran would keep going forever and ever, like some Welsh, geriatric Duracell bunny.

*

Back in our house, on lower ground, where daffodils didn't like to grow – obedient grandson that I was, I placed the egg, at the bottom of the airing cupboard. I don't know what I was expecting. At least my Gran would be pleased when I told her that I'd done it.

'It'll be 'ard boiled, you keep it b'there….temperature your Mam likes to 'ave the heating on. It'll make one hell of a scotch egg, innit?'

*

St David's Day passed, and all the days that end in y, passed and came around again. We visited my Gran again, but without all the fuss and pomp of daffodils and the weighty tins of leek soup. All the while, the egg just sat at the bottom of the airing cupboard. 'It'll all go rotten, you watch...' my Dad said. 'It'll rot away when no-one's watchin'...' I had no idea how I was meant to watch it rot away, when no-one was watching, so I just nodded and turned the heating up a click.

My Dad clicked the heating down again, instantly. I saw the colour rush to his face, I was sure I saw his dragon tattoo flex its claws...I could feel a political rant coming on. 'If you-know-who 'adn't closed all the mines in the 80s, we'd have a tidy coal fire goin' now...instead of a massive-great-big-uge heatin' bill. Bet there's loads of coal up 'ere in tha' mountain...sat 'ere, waitin' to be mined, an' now, it'll neva see the light a'day.'

*

The last words my Gran ever said to me were: 'See that old codger the other side of the corridor, the one with his zimmer, he's six years younger than me, he is! Sad innit, mun? Nevermind though, eh?' Now, I take it to mean that she loved me, and she wanted me to do well in school. So I did what any good grandson would do, and spent the next three months sitting at the back of the class, secretly playing Angry Birds on my phone.

Why should I listen to someone who had the bad manners to up and die on me without saying goodbye properly? Natural causes, my Dad said it was, though my Mam said she died of a heart attack.

'That is natural causes when you smoked as much as her,' my Dad said.

My Mam said nobody talks that way about their own mother, that my Dad didn't mean it and that it was just the grief coming out.

*

She asked for a Viking burial in her will – wanted to be put on a boat and burnt. Mind, given that the only water round by us is the reservoir, Dad said she'd have a normal cremation and like it. Mind, they did play some old rock song about fire at her funeral – Dad said he'd allow her that at least.

After her funeral, I got an envelope that I was too scared to open.

My brother got my Gran's lifetime supply of leek soup.

We all got my Gran's ashes, in an urn, that sat on the mantelpiece.

*

I sat in front of the airing cupboard and opened the doors. The egg stared back at me. I slowly ripped open the envelope. There were sheets of yellow paper inside. They smelled like nicotine and lavender. On the pages, in her shaky handwriting, she wrote: *Keep me warm. Feed me (but under no circumstances give me leek soup). Let me fly.* This time, my old Gran really had confused me.

I felt a low, soft, rumble.

All this stuff about soup and food was making me hungry.

Except, I didn't feel hungry.

The rumble wasn't coming from my stomach.

The rumble was coming from the egg.

As it cracked open, I could hear my Gran's voice in my head. I could taste every tin of leek soup she had ever given me, see every daffodil... because what came out of that egg couldn't have been more Welsh if it had come out singing Tom Jones' *Delilah*. What hatched from that egg had glistening red scales and eyes that were as green as the green, green, grass of home. What hatched from that egg, was a living breathing dragon. As it wriggled out of the egg, it destroyed the empty shell with a swish of its tail.

I heard another rumble – this time, the dragon's stomach – which was a little protruding pot-belly.

What would a dragon eat?

I heard my Gran's voice again: *I smoke to warm the cockles of my heart and keep the fire lit in my belly.*

Then my Dad's voice came booming in my ears: 'If you-know-who hadn't closed all the mines…'

Coal. I needed coal. To keep the little dragon alive, I needed to keep the fire burning in its belly. But as I watched it give a little hiccup, I saw a tiny flame that rivalled the gas hob. I checked to see that nobody was coming up the stairs; by the time I turned back, the dragon was chewing on a coat hanger. If *I* wanted to live, I needed to find this dragon some coal.

*

'Pick up your phone, mun…pick up your phone…' I spoke into my mobile. Richie's older brother had tried to do-in the jewellers on the high-street with a pick axe. He got sent down, and now Richie had some weird thing about pick-axes. He had a collection in his house that rivalled the Seven Dwarves. His parents didn't much care. Just said it was because he missed his brother. Finally he picked up the phone. 'Meet me at the top of the mountain, in half an hour. Bring a pick-axe.'

I put the dragon in my backpack – it wriggled at first, then settled – as though for a moment, it thought it was back in the egg, safe and warm. I slipped out of the door unnoticed, moving to the steady chorus of my parents arguing over the heating.

*

Pick-axe over his shoulder, trundling up the mountain, looking like every Welshman that had trundled up the mountain before him. I knew the only reason he was coming along, was so he could get his prints on the axe, so he could take the glory when the cops showed up, so he could share the cell next to his brother.

'What we looking for, then?' Richie asked.

'Coal.'

'You know Margaret Thatcher closed all the mines before we were born, right?'

'I know. Dad's still bitter about it.'

'Why the backpack? You can't put stuff you steal in a backpack. That's what duffle bags are for. My brother always told me: dufflebag, dufflebag, dufflebag.'

'I've got my dragon in it,' I said. 'The dragon my Gran gave me last St. David's Day. It needs feeding.'

There was a moment of silence.

I could feel my mobile phone ring in my pocket. Probably my parents. I decided I probably wasn't going to answer.

I could hear the nothingness on the mountain. It was a world away from the valley below with its overcrowded doctors' surgeries, boarded-up shops and the kids from the year above me mitching off school to drink cider in the park. I was above all of them. From that high up, everything looked better – the houses looked like loaves of bread, and the garden sheds looked like stacked Welsh cakes.

'Your Gran's house was round here, wasn't it?' Richie asked.

'Still is. All the other Grans and Grampas still live there.'

I found a spot and stopped dead. The grass was green, the type of green that Dylan Thomas wrote about, that they made us read in English. It looked like the sort of grass that may have escaped the clutches of Margaret Thatcher. I began to bring the pick-axe down in to the dirt. Richie sat and watched, saying nothing.

'What are you *doin'?*' he said eventually.

'Mining.'

'Yeah?' Richie said. 'I think my little brother does that when he picks his nose.'

I ignored him and laboured on, bringing the axe down hard into the harsh Welsh soil. It didn't matter how many times I brought the axe down, all I got was stones and dirt. I wondered how long it would be before I found the coal, before I unearthed the dead canaries that warned yesterday's miners of gas leaks.

My mobile phone rang in my pocket again.

Soon, I realised that there wasn't any coal, that when Margaret Thatcher closed the mines, she threw away the key as well. My shoulders burning, I threw the pick-axe down. For all Richie's brother's faults – he at least had physical strength.

'It's no good…' I panted. 'It's no good. He's going to starve.' I took the little dragon out of my backpack and he let out a long, low growl. I stared at its bejewelled green eyes. 'I'm so sorry, little dragon-guy.'

'Look…' Richie mumbled. 'I 'aven't said nothin' because I know about your gran an' all that…butt…listen now, butt… that's not a dragon, like. That's one of them Welsh Dragon Biscuit barrels in one of them egg-shaped cardboard boxes.'

'It's a real dragon, Richie.'

'It's a biscuit-tin, butt.'

'He needs fire in his belly…' I said weakly. 'He needs fire.' I reached in to the backpack and pulled a firework out.

'Hang about now…' Richie said, his eyes growing wild.

'I'll blow the coal out of the ground!' I said, feeling the fire grow in my own belly. I lit the firework and threw it with all my strength, which after the pick-axing, wasn't a lot. The firework exploded in a flash of white light and golden sparkles. It opened the earth with a thunderous crack – dirt, coal and canary bones rained down on us. I could hear my

Dad's voice, streets and streets away, shouting, 'Take that, Margaret Thatcher!'

Except none of that happened.

When it exploded, it narrowly missed Richie's leg and set the bracken alight.

There was no coal.

No canary bones.

Just me, Richie, burning bracken…and a biscuit barrel.

'My parents were arguing about the heating,' I said quietly. 'Shouting about stone cold, and things on fire… and I just had to get out.' Except they weren't arguing about the heating, they were arguing about Gran. 'She was barely cold when we had that cremation. Are you joking? Funeral parlours don't burn people alive. We can't bury her in the ground. She wanted a Viking Funeral. She's staying here with us. She wanted to be away.' I stared at the biscuit barrel in my hands. 'I had to get out. We had to get out. Me and Gran, had to get out.'

I lifted the lid on the biscuit barrel and inside, there were ashes. Gran's ashes.

Richie peeked in. 'I ain't neva seen a dead person, before like.'

I took the note out of my pocket that Gran had left.

Keep me warm, feed me, let me fly.

Let. Me. Fly.

'She liked it up here,' I said, even though I didn't think Richie was listening anymore. 'She likes all the people in her house, even if she did make fun of them. She told me once how some old lady had ended up in the flower bed in the middle of winter. Course, there were no daffs in it then. She said it was proper cold and this old woman was just standing there, starkers. Only thing with her was her handbag.'

'Christ.' Richie stared into the flames that danced on the bracken. 'That's….Christ.'

Both me and Richie knew that the fire engines were going to turn up soon. Kids always set the mountain on fire up here. My Gran's house were always callin' the fire brigade on them. My mobile phone rang in my pocket and I picked it up and threw it on the grass.

I shut the biscuit barrel one last time, and when I opened it again, the roar was so loud, that it made the birds fly from the nearby trees in fright. I could feel the tears begin to run down my cheeks. I didn't see my parents and my brother coming up the mountain behind me, barely noticed that Richie was still there. I flung the dragon in to the burning bracken. It smashed and cracked and sizzled – the dragon's green bejewelled eyes glowing in the flames.

Now, Gran was part of the mountain forever.

Now, Gran could keep the fire lit in her belly.

New Work From Previous Winners
And Commended Entrants
In The Terry Hetherington Award

Glyn Edwards

Wuthering Heights

You were exhilarated by the starkness,
marching the path past the parsonage in trim shoes
sliding over slick cobbles. Your goose-pimpled arms stretched
wider than the graveyard cedars,
'Emily's tresses would have been billowing like this,'
your tiny body a kite clapped against the draft.

The track soon shrank to wheel ruts,
then beetle brown earth, churned only by boot, by hoof.
Our steps slapped and cracked the saturated moor,
each path a gorge where rain giggled down
from the highbanking heather
and estuaried the morning's shower.

You allowed the wind to undress you,
let it press blue roses from your gown like petals,
cast them around the grey grasses, the wet white sounds,
until your colours could be found everywhere.
You saw the black grouse crash land on the gorse,
pointed out his wattle as the only red in his world,
then parsed the terminal buds by the waterfall –
the caramel yellow of a horse chestnut retreating.

The unclouded sky at the Heights was as blue as your chilled
fingers,
though a storm threatened afar like some distant sea
and a current was clinging to the air.
It drowned a man's voice nearby, choking the vowels
down his pharynx, 'Cold, in't it?'
and we trod the tumbledown timbers,
the toppled rooms, the withered ribcage,
as though scouring a beached ship exposed by low tide.

So, the photographs you took from inside the wreck,
the leaning oak centred in the frame of the stone window,
don't show the nettles growing in the kickboard
at the blown-in fireplace. They say nothing
of your damp feet, sheepshit covering them in frog spawn,
nor the fisherman's jumper you reluctantly accepted.
They tell not of your certainty, leaning on the wide
windowsill,
wildly smiling, 'I think she stood here once.'

L'Accalmie (Baie Saint-Paul)

The bleached hull, sunk now into a white-washed shore,
moored at marram grass bollards,
drifts on tides of sleep, currents of age.

Restharrow and sandwort knot it to the drydock;
only through cataract wheelhouse windows
does a visiting sea silver near.

At dusk, while distant Montreal becomes campfire coals,
this beached boat trembles again its sinewy rigging,
checks thinned charts and maps a motionless voyage.

Soon, Cassiopeia dusts a rusty mast in diamond,
the Little Fox stalks nebula towards neglected nets,
and Cygnus hurries a shoal of stars onto the deck.

The sky, a saturate of swimming light,
the boat, lulled into life by night.

*This poem responds to a photograph by Jerome Theriault,
available at the following link: http://jerometheriaultphoto.
com/2015/06/06/laccalmie/

Grace Gay

The Company of Pigeons

It's the pigeons that know her best.
They walk beside her on their cobbled
orange feet as she staggers
hand in handle around the town.

Between beakfuls of sandwich crusts
and half crushed chips, they drink
from the trails of fast cooling tea
that slip from the teapot's spout
while she roams.

Stepping over brewing puddles,
passers-by cross to other pavements
and avert their eyes
from her streak-
stained dressing gown.

Her neighbours slip their hands
through her arms, hook her in
to themselves and wearily try
to take the teapot lady home;

but the pigeons join her coos
as she continues her search for George.

Birmingham Underpass

The only light is the cat's eyes.
Their eyelids blink
against the tread of your tyres
as your gaze rests
on the threading lines
of the road ahead.

The walls grow darker,
lined by fumes,
hemming in the smell of warm tar –
you could be anywhere.

Time could be going backwards
in the city above you,
the tightly knit buildings
could unravel at the seams
spreading into sheets,
but you're still moving on.

You slow down
to savour
the spaces between the city –
the hidden parts
of a pin

running
beneath the fabric
to secure it in place.

Molly Jamieson

Melissa the Magnificent

'Pick a card, any card,' she said.

She fanned the deck out in her hands, and offered it to him over the bread basket.

'My dear Melissa,' he said, 'you really have no feel for timing. Why, for dinnertime magic, one must at least have selected the hors d'oeuvres.'

'Hors d'oeuvres?' She de-fanned the cards and replaced the deck in her bag. 'If you say so.'

'I do say so.'

'Well, then,' she said, raising her glass, 'here's to timing.'

Melissa had been dating The Incredible Gavin for three months to the day, but try as she may her attempts to enter his world of magic had always been rebuffed. He was as skilled a one-upper as he was a magician, and it was his chief delight to demonstrate it.

When she produced a coin from behind his ear, he produced a string of handkerchiefs from her sleeve. When she asked him to guess which cup the ball was hidden under, he answered 'all of them' and was right, despite her having the solitary ball *she* had employed for the trick stowed in her hand. When she produced a rabbit from a hat, he took the hat from her and, with a tap from his wand, conjured ten doves.

Now, her flat was spattered with bird shit, her arms were

covered with rabbit bites, and she had had enough. She was going to show him a trick that would surprise even The Incredible Gavin.

The waiter appeared, as if by magic, and glanced once at His Incredibleness, who had come straight from work, without time to change. The glance was enough to take in Gavin's top hat, purple and black silk bow-tie, cape, and waistcoat, with the silver medal he had won at the Derbyshire County Best Magician Competition 2009 pinned to the lapel, before the waiter turned his gaze to Melissa.

'May I take your order?' he said.

'You know, I haven't even checked the menu yet,' she said. She took it from the centre of the table, and found herself holding a blank piece of paper. 'Gavin.'

'Sorry, darling, still at work in my mind.' As always, she mused. 'Here you are.'

She took it and it crumbled into glitter. *'Gavin.'*

'Sorry, darling, work work work, you know. It's stuck to the bottom of your chair.'

She reached under her seat and pulled it out. Relieved to see that it was the real menu, she began to peruse. Gavin fixed his attention on the waiter.

'I'll have the *soupe à l'oignon*, and the *tuna niçoise* main. Darling?'

'The bruschetta,' she said, and handed the menu to the waiter.

'And for the main?'

'No main for me.'

'No main?'

'No.'

'OK. I'll bring those over. It should only be a few minutes.'

'Thanks.'

Silence settled over the couple. The Incredible Gavin selected a bread roll from the basket and proceeded to butter it.

Melissa went to take a gulp of her wine, before she realised that the glitter faux-menu had shed into her glass, and set it aside.

'How about my trick, then?' she said. 'Unless the timing is still off.'

'No, this'll do.'

'OK, then.' She pulled out the deck and offered it to him as before. 'Pick a card, any card.'

He stifled a sigh at her use of such common magical jargon, but, in the spirit of being a good sport, did as instructed, and picked a card.

On seeing it, he frowned. His mouth opened.

'Don't tell me,' she interrupted quickly. 'Memorise it, and replace it in the deck.'

A little shaky, he obeyed.

'Melissa,' he said.

She shuffled the deck, and gave him a questioning glance. 'Mm?'

'My card...'

'Don't tell me.'

He closed his mouth. She continued to shuffle. 'Now pick a number between one and fifty.'

'Fifty?' he said. 'Don't you mean fifty-two?'

'No, this deck is special in that way. And other ways. Pick a number between one and fifty.'

'I –' He paused. 'One.'

She took the top card and showed it to him. 'Was this your card?'

On the table between them lay the card, which read, in cursive script, *I'm breaking up with you.*

He shook his head. 'No,' he said, breathing heavily. 'Mine said 'It just isn't working out between us'.'

'Well, it was close enough,' she said. She dropped the cards on the table and he saw that there were only two types of card, both with those rather similar messages.

'But why?'

'Oh, Gavin, I like you a lot. I just can't handle the magic any more. I'm sorry. Somehow it's become our entire lives, but you never let me have a part in it.'

He sniffed and nodded slowly, his eyes downcast. 'I wanted you to be my assistant,' he said.

'I know,' she said fondly, 'but we both agreed that wasn't a good idea, after you tried to saw me in half and I had to get stitches. Remember?'

'I remember,' he said. 'It took weeks to get the blood out of the carpet.'

They laughed quietly together, engaged in happy memory.

The waiter returned with the starters and placed them on the table. Melissa took a bite of her bruschetta.

'Besides,' added The Incredible Gavin, scattering croutons into his soup, 'you never really had a flair for magic.'

Melissa swallowed her mouthful. 'Well…You never let me,' she said.

'Let you?'

'You never let me win one,' she said. 'Whenever I tried to learn a trick for you, you always showed me up.'

'I wasn't showing you up,' he scoffed. 'I was trying to teach you.'

'Teach me? You never explained a single trick to me!'

'I wasn't teaching you tricks, I was trying to teach you *flair*. Of course I didn't tell you my secrets, what do you think I am, some kind of amateur?'

Melissa slammed down her fork. '*Yes!*'

They stared at each other in silent outrage, which was only broken when Gavin shoved his hand into his soup, scooped up a handful of onions and croutons, and threw it down on the floor.

There was a sudden poof of smoke that masked him, and

when it cleared he had vanished.

Melissa glanced around the restaurant, unable to find the speedily fleeing purple cloak, able only to find astonished stares.

She sat still for a moment in exasperated silence, until she heard gentle sobs coming from under the table. 'Oh, Gavin,' she said.

Sighing, she took a twenty-pound note from her purse and dropped it beside her plate, on top of her special deck of cards.

'I'll come by tomorrow and pick up my stuff from your flat,' she said, rising.

She gathered her things and walked out.

*

When Melissa arrived home, there was a package outside her door. She carried it inside and laid it on the kitchen island. It was taped shut with a note, 'For Melissa'.

She took a knife and cut it open. It was full of her books and clothes, things she had left at Gavin's flat.

On top of the neatly arranged pile was a small jewellery box, only big enough to hold a ring.

'Oh, god,' she said, and opened it.

A cascade of glitter tumbled out onto the parcel, leaving only a small note inside.

She read:

Alakazam, bitch.

Melissa sighed, shook her head, and took a step back from the counter.

And the parcel burst into flame.

Tyler Keevil

Fishhook

My lure hit the water with a satisfying plop. I locked the reel and waited until the tip of my rod bent from the weight. Then I pulled back on the rod, eased up, and reeled in. You have to pull gently and not yank because yanking makes the lure look all wrong, and the fish can sense something fake in how it moves. To attract them the bacon fat should sort of flap in the water, fluttering along like a moth with busted wings, because that's what bullheads want. Dale explained it to me one time. He said, 'Bullies like to bite stuff that looks maimed and hurt. That's the trick.' I've never really understood why, but it works. I guess it's instinct.

'Nice cast,' Dale said.

We were fishing where we always fish: on this old wharf near Port Moody, way the hell out at the end of Burrard Inlet. The water was still choppy, slopping at the pontoons, and the pilings of the dock creaked and groaned like an old man's bones. Evening was coming on and a few crows shrieked from among the sycamores that lined the shore. The dock isn't too far from the city, but it's far enough that you still feel like you're getting back to nature when you're down there. No people, no cars, no bullshit. Just this primal sort of feeling. I figure that's part of what makes fishing such a thrill.

On my first cast I didn't catch anything, and neither did Dale. That was typical. The bullheads aren't usually interested right away. You got to get their attention, first. I reared back and leaned into the next cast. The lure sailed out a long way before I heard the slap of lead and bacon on water.

'Beer up,' Dale said.

I took the can of Lucky he offered me and began reeling in.

*

I got the first bite. I don't know what's it like to catch a big fish, but with bullheads sometimes you can't tell they're on the line. You feel the resistance and your rod bends like a bow. Maybe you're hooked in weeds, or snagged on a rock – it's hard to say. Then, when you give it a tug, the rod starts trembling and nipping up and down like a needle on one of those lie detectors.

'Got one.'

I said it like it didn't matter but it did.

When you're reeling in, you got to keep the tension on the line or you'll lose the fish. I never use a barbed hook on account it hurts them – gets stuck in their mouths too easy, and tears when you pull it out. I use plain hooks, but without a barb you need that tension or the fish can slip off if he's cagey enough. Bullies aren't very cagey, but once in a while you get one with some savvy. Dale doesn't have to worry about that, because he uses barbed hooks.

'Ain't a goer,' I said. 'Fight's gone out of him.'

I could see a white shaft sliding up through the water to meet me. Sometimes the littler ones do that – they go all limp and passive so it isn't any fun. It's like playing with yourself or something. Fishing is supposed to be a two-sided sort of exercise.

157

It cleared the water and got lighter without the drag.

'Aww, man,' I said. 'Just a baby.'

'Still a catch.'

'It's barely bigger than the bacon.'

Dale snickered. 'Bit off more'n he can chew.'

We never keep the fish we catch, but even so I don't like hooking the babies. I think it's kind of unfair, seeing as how they're so young and all. I mean, where's the sport in that? Dale doesn't care one way or the other. He always says, 'Thrill's just the same to me.'

Dale's funny like that.

I scooped the fish up with my left hand. I hate that part most of all and wanted to get it done quick. The fish thrashed about and I had to tighten my grip so as not to lose him. I was working the hook out of the mouth when Dale's rod dipped sharp towards the water.

'Got one,' he said.

*

After that things picked up. Usually we nab about half a dozen bullheads each by the time night drops her skirt and they stop biting. But the fish were acting crazy that day and we hooked at least that many in the first hour.

'This is really weird,' I kept saying. 'Man, this is weird.'

And Dale would reply, 'These fish are going loco, man.'

I think loco is Spanish for crazy. I took it up on my tongue, because it's one of those words you like to roll around inside your mouth. 'Yeah,' I'd say, 'these fish are *loco*, man.'

But mostly we didn't have time to say anything except, 'Got another.' After the first one it was always, 'Got another.' We kept saying that until we didn't even have to do much more than grunt and the other would understand.

At one point I started thinking about how many bullheads

were in the water. I always figured that after you hooked one and let it go, it would shoot off and go hide someplace. But we'd caught at least twenty, maybe thirty bullies so far that night. It seemed like too many.

'You think these fish are all new ones?'

I could tell Dale hadn't considered it because he didn't answer straight away.

'Reckon so. Wouldn't make sense to come back for more, would it? Even bullies ain't that stupid.'

'Yeah. Reckon so.'

'Seems like an awful lot of fish, though.'

'That's what I thought.'

We were both poised with our weight on one foot, ready to cast. But we didn't.

Dale said, 'Maybe we could find out.'

I looked at him. Even before he told me, I'd cottoned on to what he had in mind. It made a kind of sense. We'd been stapling posters all day – my uncle had paid us to put them up on notice boards and telephone poles around town, advertising his landscaping company. The big industrial stapler he'd lent us was still in my car, back at the parking lot.

I was the one who went to get it.

*

I would hold the fish and Dale would staple them. We figured the best place to do it was between the spines of the dorsal fin. There's this thin skin between the spines, like the webbing on a frog's feet, and when we clipped a staple there the bullies didn't even seem to notice. Dale said it would be like the tags you see those scientists using to track whales or dolphins or whatever. This way, we'd be able to tell if we'd caught a fish before. It worked, too. We'd only tagged eight or nine fish before I caught one that already had a staple. I held my rod upright, so the fish dangled at eye level. He was as thick as a fist, and about ten or twelve inches long. That's pretty sizeable for a bully.

'I remember him,' Dale said. 'It's that big mother I caught first.'

'Looks like it.'

'What a dimwit.' Dale flicked its belly with his finger. 'You stupid dimwit.'

'Let's double him up,' I said.

Dale wrested the dimwit off the hook and turned him sideways so I could clip a second staple behind the first. Then Dale hucked him. He grabbed him by the tail and just threw him, high and far in the air. He splashed into the water on his back.

'Last can of Lucky says he comes back for more.'

'I don't know, man,' I said.

'Come on.'

I didn't care about the bet, or the beer. I would've given it to Dale if he'd asked. I just didn't like how Dale said it – as if it meant something. But I knew how he could get.

'Okay,' I said.

We plunked our lures back into the water. Then we both stood silent, thinking.

'Maybe they don't have such hot memories,' I said.

'Why would that matter?'

'My uncle told me goldfish only remember things for seven seconds. That's why they never get bored swimming around in circles. Maybe bullies are the same.'

'Maybe.'

Dale didn't sound convinced.

'What, then?'

He didn't answer. His line jerked once and he had another. I stopped jigging and let my own rod go limp to watch him reel in. The fish came out, trembling and flicking its tail, and Dale waited for it to settle. This one was smaller, but its fin was already stapled, too.

'Got me another gobbler,' Dale said.

I tried to make some joke about these fish being *really* loco, but Dale wasn't having any of it. He didn't say much after that first big one came back, and even less after it came back a second time. There must have only been about twenty fish out there, all taking turns to chomp down on our lures. We stapled a dozen of them twice, and then a few others three or four times. Most of all we stapled the big one – the one Dale called Dimwit. With Dimwit we had to stop using the stapler after seven times, because there was no more room on his fin.

Dale always put the staple in. He wanted to. He said he liked it. I was the opposite, but I didn't say anything as I held the fish for him. I just cupped them cold and slick in my hands and wondered what they wanted, these fish that kept coming back for more.

*

'I know – these fish ain't so dumb, after all. They're pretty smart, right Dale? I mean, they know we throw them back, so they figure it's okay to keep on being caught since they get a bit of bacon for all the trouble. Man, these fish aren't loco. They're real savvy, right?'

Dale wasn't listening. He was crouched down, fiddling with his hook. The sun had slid down behind the mountains, and the waves had settled, and the inlet had gone all dark and lonesome and still. Most of the fish had stopped biting. That wasn't why I'd given up casting awhile back, though. I'd caught so many bullies I'd had a belly-full by then. I was beginning to feel as if I was the one who'd eaten all that bait, not them.

'Gonna try it without any bacon,' Dale said.

It took me a second to figure out what he meant.

'That won't work,' I said. 'Even a bullhead isn't as stupid as that.'

Dale just shrugged. I started packing up our stuff. I put the lures in the tackle box, flipped shut the lid, and snapped the clasps in place. Then I squatted down on it and waited with my rod lying limp across my lap. Dale lifted his own rod high, stiff and straight, before whipping it forward. Line whizzed from the reel, and the hook traced a long, loping arc that disappeared into the murk. A second later the splunk of the weight on water came back to us.

'I want to go, Dale. They're not biting any more.'

'He'll bite.'

We waited. All the crows had gone quiet. A breeze rustled the sycamores and stirred the surface of the water. In the distance you could hear a siren whining, but that was the only sign of the city. We peered into the water and the dark. You couldn't tell which was which by then, since they seemed to blend together out there. Dale's lips were half-parted and he was breathing through his mouth. Every time he inhaled there was this sucking noise, eager and hungry, like somebody sipping hot soup. That happens sometimes, when Dale gets excited, on account of the asthma he had as a kid.

'No fish is gonna bite a bare hook,' I said. It didn't make any sense. I mean, you snag them sometimes – in a gill or under a fin – but that's different. 'Even if they got no memory, and can't remember, why in the hell would they bite a hook without any bait?'

'Maybe they do remember. Maybe it ain't the bait they like.'

I had a think about that. I was hugging myself, even though it wasn't really cold.

'Course it's the bait. It has to be the bait.'

Then Dale grunted, in the way we did when we'd got a bite, but this time it was different. It was closer to a groan – as if he'd tasted something sweet, or seen a pretty girl.

He began reeling in. The tip of his rod bent low towards the water, but there was no tugging or fight in the line. I figured it was just a snag. Something that big had to be a snag, or else it wouldn't have been so willing. Then the white shape rose up from the depths like a torpedo and breached the surface.

'It's him,' Dale said. 'It's Dimwit.'

Dale hoisted him up, and held the line steady as he stroked the belly-flesh with his forefinger. He cooed at it like a lover. The fish blinked and puckered its mouth repeatedly, sucking at the air. Between its soft, rubbery lips, I could see the gleaming barb of the hook.

Anna Lewis

Boxing Day Matinée

It was the first time in four years that the sisters had spent Christmas together, and at the moment she answered the door, Lyn was unable to think what to say. Kate smiled in the doorway, Gareth looming cheerily behind her. Lyn hoped that she was smiling back.

Four years since she had met Ahmet on a wet winter's evening, after she had ordered a Chinese take-away and opened a bottle of wine. That night, she had drunk several glasses by the time the doorbell rang. He had stood where Kate and Gareth were standing now. Water clotted his hair and ran down his cheeks, darkened the tops of his shoulders and the bottoms of his jeans. He apologised: he had got lost looking for her flat. He shivered as he spoke and Lyn, warmed through with wine, said, 'Come in if you like. Dry off for a bit.'

'I can't,' he said, 'the shop,' but she stood aside and held open the door, and with a wide, silly grin he wiped his feet on the mat and walked past her, into the hallway.

He was Turkish, and two years younger than she was. He did not stay long that evening, but he ate some of her food, and asked for her mobile number before he left. He called her a few days later. On Tuesdays the take-away was closed, and he picked her up in a car that smelt of garlic and sweet-and-sour sauce. They drove to the coast, and leaned into each other as they walked along the promenade, wind railing in off the sea. Rapid clouds surrounded the moon, and white foam cut the surface of the water far out into the mouth of the bay. When she couldn't stop herself from shivering, he laughed and put an arm around her shoulders, and guided her towards the pier. In a café with plastic chairs fixed to the floor, they ate fish and chips and drank fizzy pop, before he drove her home. They married a month later, a week before Christmas.

It was a small, registry office wedding. On Lyn's side was one old friend from her university days – none of her other friends had been able to get time off work at such short notice, and so close to Christmas – and Kate, then a student herself. Her parents had refused to come. They were very upset, Kate said; they could not understand what she was doing, and feared that she was being taken for a ride by someone who 'is just out to get permanent residency, or something, Dad says.'

'But Ahmet doesn't want permanent residency – he wants to go back to Turkey, once he's saved up a bit more money.'

The anxiety on Kate's face twisted into anguish. 'So does that mean you're going to Turkey with him?'

Lyn had not thought about it. They had not discussed it. Ahmet's parents were, apparently, also very upset about the marriage – not, as Lyn had first imagined, because they minded him marrying a British girl, but because there had not been enough time for them to arrange to travel to the wedding. Ahmet's only guests were the middle-aged Chinese couple who owned the take-away, and their two teenage daughters. As a wedding present they had laid on a dim sum buffet for the reception in Lyn's flat. They had catered for twenty people, and seemed horribly embarrassed. After they had left the reception, Lyn packed up the mounds of leftover food and tried to give it to Kate. 'Go on,' she said, 'share it with your house-mates – take it.'

Kate shook her head until tears came into her eyes. 'I don't even like Chinese food,' she said. 'I don't know why you do. I wish you didn't.'

Christmas Eve passed, and Christmas Day. Boxing Day grew dark. They had left a light on in Lyn's hallway, glowing in the frosted glass of her front door, and in the passenger seat Kate turned around, resting her hand on Gareth's knee. They were not far from the theatre; blue and white lights were strung across every street. 'I forgot to tell you, Lyn,' she said. 'We're meeting someone there, a friend of ours.'

'We are?'

'Our friend Ross. He's ever so nice.' Kate tucked a strand of hair behind her ear, an old nervous habit.

'Why have you invited him?'

'Oh, you know... he got divorced last year, and it's not a nice time of year to be alone...'

Lyn sighed and sank back into her seat.

By the time they arrived the lobby was hot and crowded, and muggy with the scent of mulled wine. Battered foil Christmas decorations hung limply from the ceiling. Gareth queued at the bar, and at Lyn's insistence the sisters went to stand close to the doors, where cold air charged in every time someone entered. Kate kept looking around at the clogged foyer, and after a couple of minutes began to smile. A tall man in a soft grey shirt was pushing politely through the crowd towards them. 'Kate,' he said when he reached their spot by the door. He kissed Kate on the cheek and turned to Lyn. 'You must be Lynette. I'm Ross.' He held out a hand. 'Can I get you a drink – both of you?'

'Gareth is already getting them, thank you,' said Lyn.

Ross looked disappointed. Kate started to talk, and as Ross answered Lyn stepped back to let her gaze slide across

166

the lobby. There were more children than she had expected, more people altogether. Gareth returned with three glasses of mulled wine. There was some awkwardness, and Ross went alone to the bar to get a drink for himself.

The play was a comedy, with songs. Kate and Gareth laughed a lot, loudly, and Gareth occasionally began to sing along, but each time Kate smacked him lightly on the thigh or the arm until he stopped. Ross sat beside Lyn, and laughed gently in the right places, and did not sing, and did not speak to Lyn or even look in her direction. During the interval Lyn took herself to the ladies' loos, where there were only three cubicles and the queue ran out into the corridor and up the stairs; by the time she returned to her seat, the second half was about to begin.

After the play was over, Gareth led the four of them in a line along the row of seats and down the staircase into the foyer. 'Thank you Kate, thank you Gareth,' said Lyn. 'That was fun. Nice to have met you, Ross.' She took a step towards the door, but Ross cleared his throat and said hastily, 'Why don't we – would you like to come for a drink, Lyn? We didn't have much chance to – ' He glanced at Gareth and Kate, and blushed. Gareth and Kate began a sudden, earnest conversation, turning to face the doors.

Lyn was embarrassed on Ross's behalf, but she shook her head. 'We've got to get back, I'm sorry,' she said. In an instant Gareth and Kate were facing them again, Kate batting a hand in the air. 'Don't worry about us, you two – if you don't mind lending us the key, Lyn, we're quite happy to go back on our own – '

'It's no trouble,' said Gareth.

Lyn was hot, the small of her back ached from the uncomfortable seat, she was surrounded by crowds and children; she was being made to humiliate a man whom she did not know, and of whom she had no opinion. 'Thank you, I would just like to go home,' she said. 'Goodbye, Ross.' She crossed the foyer and pushed through the doors into the car park.

No one spoke during the drive back to the flat. Gareth whistled songs from the show and Kate stared straight ahead. Once inside, Lyn drew the curtains and put the kettle on to boil. Gareth, who said that mulled wine did not agree with him, went to lie down in the spare room. The two sisters sat in armchairs in front of the empty fireplace, mugs of tea on a low table between them.

'I thought you might like Ross,' said Kate, after a while. 'It was my idea. He's Gareth's friend really, and I pushed him to come.'

'I didn't not like him,' said Lyn. 'I didn't think anything of him at all.'

'I should have told you sooner.'

'You just shouldn't have done it. I don't need you match-making me.'

In her chair, Kate seemed to reduce a little. 'It just seems such a waste, you being on your own,' she said quietly.

'I'm fine on my own. I'm happy. I don't understand the problem. When I was with someone you hated it, now I'm alone you won't let me be –'

'With someone? The Turkish bloke?'

'Ahmet.'

'You were hardly *with* him, that was – I've had one night stands that have lasted longer than that marriage.'

'Don't be disgusting – and anyway, why is that, do you think? You made me feel so guilty, did you know I cried myself to sleep on my own wedding night because of you?'

'Well, what does that tell you?'

Kate and Gareth left the following day, after breakfast. Lyn hugged them both, Gareth briefly and out of politeness, but she wrapped her arms around Kate and squeezed her. 'Come back soon,' she said. 'It was fun having you here. It's nice to have guests.'

'Come to ours,' said Kate, into Lyn's shoulder. 'I'd love to have you.'

'I will, I'll come soon.' She stood on the step and waved as they drove away down the street, pulling her cardigan across her chest against the cold.

It was about six o'clock in the evening when the telephone rang. She was running a bath, and carried the cordless receiver into the bathroom as she answered. She clutched the phone to her ear with one hand and held the other under the tap to test the water. 'Hello?'

The voice at the other end was indistinct, and she sighed slightly as she turned the tap off, before repeating, 'Hello?'

'Hello – is that Lynette?' It was a man's voice, nervous, and one she didn't recognise.

'Who is this?'

'It's Ross – I'm sorry, it's Ross: we met at the theatre yesterday.'

'Oh – yes.' She looked down at the shallow, swaying water in the tub, and frowned.

'I'm sorry to trouble you, Lynette – I spoke to Gareth earlier, as it happens, I asked him for your number – I hope you don't mind. The thing is, I'm sorry that we didn't get much chance to speak yesterday. I didn't get to buy you a drink...'

He paused, and Lyn listened, saying nothing. Ross cleared his throat and continued. 'I know that you probably didn't get much impression of me yesterday – but the thing is – I would like to take you for a proper drink. I think – perhaps we could try to get to know each other. Just a little.'

He paused again and, as she had in the foyer the previous afternoon, Lyn felt embarrassed for him. 'Ross,' she said, 'of course I don't mind Gareth giving you my number. But we don't really know anything about each other, do we? I don't know if there's much to be gained –'

He interrupted her, his voice stronger, more urgent. 'But that's what I mean. We don't know each other, but when I met you yesterday, I just had a feeling that – if we did – we might get on. It's just a chance I know, but – come for a drink with me, Lynette.'

'I don't – '

'– It's just a chance. Come for one drink with me. One drink can't hurt.'

She sat down, slowly, on the edge of the bath. 'Alright,' she said softly, 'one drink. Okay.' She seemed to hear him smile.

Once the call was over and she had replaced the receiver in its cradle, she began to run the tap again, took off her clothes, and hung them on the back of the door. As the room warmed, the wall grew clammy with steam but she stood leaning against it, watching her reflection blur in the mirror on the opposite side of the room.

It was four years since she had accepted an invitation from a man, four years since she had gone to bed with a man. She thought that she would telephone him in the morning and cancel. She thought of Kate sitting by the fireplace, staring down at the hearth, thought of Kate's bony shoulders as they had hugged on the step that morning. She climbed into the tub and lowered herself inch by inch until she was lying on her back, her knees drawn up, her head resting on the edge.

One drink can't hurt. Of course it could. It was always the small steps that mattered most: because you took so many more of them: because, once you tried to go back, there were so many more to undo. But these thoughts were endless once they had begun, and in the hot water she was growing drowsy. The soap was at the other end of the bath, by the taps, and she shuffled onto her knees, reached an arm out through the steam.

170

Joâo Morais

The Forage

This is how you gets free class As for life. At the end of October, go for a drive until the ground is more green than grey. Hop over the nearest fence, check there's no mad horny animals around that might want to bum you, then look at the floor. If you can't see nothing but grass and cowdumps in the first ten seconds, go find another field.

What you're looking for is these little hooded beige mushrooms. You knows you got the right ones if their crooked stems look too flimsy to hold up their heads. These little blowers are more powerful than anything you will ever get that was made in some Dutch laboratory. And if you knows what you're doing all they'll ever cost you is enough for your petrol money and a pack of smokes.

It's like your Nana always told you. The best things in life are free. Don't pay for shoes. There's about fifty pairs waiting for you outside every Mosque. Don't pay for cocaine. Just give yourself a semi and walk around your house like your dick was at its normal size. Don't pay for an electric toothbrush. Just get your old toothbrush and tape it to your girlfriend's dildo.

I takes my new Mrs to my special field. It's up this mountain from where you can see the Millennium Stadium and the Severn Bridge and half the Somerset coast. After going past the rugby club, we turns right and goes through the suburb with the nice semi-detached houses with their polished front gardens. Then we goes on to the single-track road at the back of the estate that takes us halfway up mushroom mountain.

If you finds a good spot, don't tell no twonkey about it. For every person you tells, expect them to tell their spars and then them to tell their spars. Before you know it every joker from Pentwyn to Gabalfa is raping your patch raw. Just like the ones everyone knows about up Mynydd Rudry or by the big water fountain at the top of Pentrebane.

Grabbing mushrooms for a brew is one of the most fun things you can do outdoors. Go with someone you got a thing for and it heightens all the feelings you got for them. Cat my new Mrs don't half look the part. She makes green wellies and a brown waterproof jacket look as sexy as any other bird would a push-up bra and edible knickers.

I gets to the summit about three minutes before her cos I'm so excited. When she gets to the top, her cheeks are all flushed and her hair is in her face and I could bang her right here and now. She rests on the floor and rolls a smoke. I pumps out some three-finger one-armed press ups, just to keep the blood flowing. And just in case she wants to notice how hot I'm looking right now.

I tells her the basics as we goes along. If you doesn't have much in the way of experience, take someone along with you for the trip. And that means the trip up the mountain but also the trip into the deepest darkest bits of your swede. That's the bit where all the things you doesn't know you're thinking about are hiding. It's dangerous to go there on your own.

If you spies a mushroom but doesn't trust it, then you shouldn't eat it. If it's got white gills underneath the hood then it could be a poisonous impostor that wants to blind you. Some types of mushroom are so bad that before you knows it your piss stings every time you go and you're on eight hours of dialysis a day for the rest of your life. Mushrooms are pretty hardcore and they got a rep about them for a reason. But don't be a Mary about it. Picking is one of those milestones in life, like passing your car test or having your first spliff or threesome. As soon as you've done it, at no matter what age, no-one really cares. You've joined the club.

Cat is a natural. Her eyes are sharper than festival scrumpy. She got the kind of gaze where you half wants to take her in the summer to the Glasto litter-pick when it is all over, just to see what drugs and wallets she finds.

Within a half hour, we each got most of a salad bag full. You has to get as much as you can, so you can cover your own use and any you needs to sell out of season. The twonkeys who think they're above you just cos they can afford to camp for three days in their own shit to see some has-been bands don't half go mad for some overpriced organic fungi. Just remember to never uproot them. They're called magic mushrooms for a reason. They grows new heads if you leaves the roots in. And also remember to flick before you pick. That way, all the spores gets freed, so there's more around to sell to the twonkeys next year and all.

We been there a couple of hours and we're proper getting in to the swing of things. You knows you're doing well when you starts seeing the little nippers everywhere, and you has to chuck your water bottle at one patch, your jumper at another, and you even has to take off a shoe to chuck at a pile in case they disappears.

Then I looks over at Cat and I notices that she ain't helping. She ain't really done much since I told her to think like a mushroom. Maybe she don't understand. If you can't see anything then crouch down to their level and look at your new horizon. Come back and tell me of the mad things you can see down there. She musta took it all too serious and went blank inside as if she were growing out the side of the mountain herself. Or maybe she just got a bit peckish and decided to have a munch. She's watching me chuck mushrooms into a plastic bag but she ain't got no smile on her face.

I walks over and sits down next to her. – Wassamarra luv? I says.

She wants to say something but it just ain't coming out. You knows the feeling. It's the same when you waits to spew. First you has to wait for your body to be ready before it lets you splash your guts all over the floor. It's always the first retch that brings up the most, filling your mouth and nose with that hot sour acid of whatever you were drinking. She's at that stage where she knows it will do her good and it will make her feel better afterwards, but she's still dribbling and holding her hair back before the next wave comes.

She turns to face me. Her eyebrows raise up in the middle as she grabs my hands.

– I think we run into this too soon, she says.

She looks less nervous straight away, even when she looks at the floor. But what her face can't hide is what her voice really wants to say. Cos what it's really saying is, I think I run into this too soon.

The signs were always there. I pulls my hands away and pulls out two smokes. – I'm sorry you feels that way, I says back.

She sparks up her smoke with her own lighter. – It's just, I wish I could have met you at a different stage of my life.

She breathes out and looks at Church Village at the foot of the mountain. She's at one of those in-between stages of life, where you're being tested and you're not sure who you're turning into.

It's one of those things that you sees every now and again

174

in people of a certain age who don't quite know how to think about life. Think about the last porn starlet you wanked over. When you saw her first video she was all nervous and raw and it all seemed real. She was getting smashed by some real man for the first time. A pro twice her age with a torso like pillar who has been through a million girls like her before.

Two years, eight tattoos and a hundred scenes later and she's moaning on cue like the rest of them. You couldn't get proper stiff for her even if she was spreading her cheeks in front of you. All her dead peepers are able to think of is the big pearly rock she'll be smoking later when she cashes her paycheque in some backdoor pawnshop. She's forgotten who she was and is probably two bong hits and an injection away from a cardiac arrest.

Catrin is at that early stage and she don't wanna end up like no porn starlet. Some things you has to learn for yourself, like just cos you keeps your phone in your back pocket it don't mean you're gonna get arse cancer.

I takes a drag and looks at all our stuff spread over the place, knowing that each one is next to a big juicy pile of mushrooms. – Don't worry, love. Plenty of time to get to know each other.

She takes in a drag and breathes it out as she speaks. – I still feel I have so much of the world to see.

It's lucky when you had enough birds to know when they wants reassurance, even if you ain't learnt this one's menstrual cycle yet. – It's all good, love. You moved away from home, you gone to College, you're doing OK, you are.

– Not like tha, she says. – Easy for you, it is. Youer a bloke.

I raises my eyebrows and takes a drag to think of the right answer. – I doesn't know what you means.

She gives you a little laugh as she sits up a bit straighter. – I bet you given this whole spiel to loadsa women up here.

I feels like I'm out of tricks. I coughs twice, even though

175

all it can do is buy three seconds more time. – Not at all, love. I only ever brought you up to this special place. And I ain't been with that many birds anyhow.

She turns to face me. The way her eyelids close slightly around the bright green of her peepers lets you know that she is expecting the right answer. – Well how many women have you been with en?

It had to come sooner or later. The question with no right answer. Too low and you're a dud. Too high and you might have AIDS. I pull a figure out of my arse. It's about half what the real number is.

She chokes and looks away. – Tell me youer joken. Tha must be youer idea of a joke.

It don't matter what I says next, cos before I get any words out I swallows and moves my hand as if I'm gonna put a smoke in my mouth. – Oh love, don't be like that. I am a few years older than you. Don't forget, you woulda just been in high school by the time I shoulda been doin my GCSE.

She flicks half a smoke away, even though she knows not to piss the farmer off by leaving any rubbish. – I carn believe that so many women have meant so much to you. I'll be waiten for you by the car.

She gets up and starts marching her arse up the hill so she can go down the other side where the car is parked. I can't help but let out a little laugh when she says about all the other birds, even though I curses after cos she more than likely heard it. Cos the truth is most of those birds meant fuck all.

I leans over and grabs the smoke she left. As I finishes it off, I has one of those moments where you comes to some realisation you shoulda got to ages ago. The number I gave her, I probably shoulda halved it again.

You always got to think ahead. A cow will lie down on the grass when it's about to rain so she still got a nice dry bit to eat. And that's when it all clicks. When she split with her last guy,

176

she didn't want me. She just wanted an ending.

I gives her five minutes to cool off by going to collect all the stuff we chucked around, collecting each patch of little nippers they are next to as I goes along. A small dose of mushrooms and it affects your body like you taken a dab of MDMA. You kinda wish that things didn't go tits up so you coulda taken a few and had a bubble on the way back down the hill.

I gets to the car and she's leaning on it, arms crossed. She won't look at me and she's never looked so beautiful.

– There's still bare mushrooms up there, I says to break the silence. – We got to get them before the hippies come and raid this place.

She smooths the lining of my coat between her forefinger and thumb. Anything but to look at me. – OK, cariad, she says. – But I wanna go home now. Forget about all I said up there.

She finally gives me a smile as I chucks over the keys so she can open up her door. I has a good look at her face again when I'm sat down in the seat next to her. All she ever bothers with is mascara and lip balm so normally you can clock the mood on her face like you can clock the mood of the weather. But this time it's different. She's giving you a smile you've seen on the occasional bird before. It's the same one that your mum mighta given you once when you was a nipper and she accidentally left the fire on all night and locked all the doors on Christmas Eve, and Father Crimbo couldn't get in to leave no presents under the tree.

You both knows what's going on but you has to play along or the other person will start bawling. All that Cat's eyes can tell is half the story. All they can tell you is that behind the smile on that pretty clear face is everything you will never understand.

Thomas Morris

The First Time I Met My Father

The first time I met my father he was wearing a cowboy hat.

'My long lost son,' he said, arms outstretched like brackets.

'Howdie,' I replied.

He bought us drinks and got me drunk. He told me stories about my mother and all the other women he'd had kids with.

'I don't remember yours that well,' he said. 'Tell me, does she have a mole on her bum?'

I told him I didn't know and he looked non-plussed.

At the end of the night he gave me a hug and said he'd enjoyed himself.

'Let's do this again some time,' he said.

'Yeah,' I said. 'It's been a delight.'

The second time I met my father he was wearing a Welsh rugby top and a pair of jeans. We were outside the Millenium Stadium.

'I used to play,' he said.

'Any good?' I replied.

'Fucking useless.'

We watched the game and he was the loudest person in our part of the crowd. Children stared at him, afraid. The whole game he screamed like a lunatic.

When we left he apologised for the scoreline.

'I honestly thought we were going to win today,' he said.

We said goodbye at Central train station, and I watched him disappear into a crowd of middle-aged men.

The third time I met my father he was wearing a smile the width of his face.

'This is Pamela,' he said, gesturing at the blonde woman beside him. She wore a purple top with a silver dollar sign across the front.

He bought us dinner and boasted about his travels.

'But in the end, the places all the places start to look the same. Honest to god, Arizona isn't that different to Merthyr.'

I told him that I'd never been abroad and he laughed.

'I must take you sometime,' he said. Pamela grinned at me the whole time, as if I was some physical evidence of his abilities as a man.

'As always, it's been a pleasure,' he said, and he and Pamela rose from the table, waved goodbye from the taxi.

The fourth time I met my father we argued about money.

'But my dad gave me fuck all,' he said.

'I only need a little bit,' I said. 'I'm just short on rent.'

'It's immoral,' he said. 'A man should make his own way in the world.'

'And that's why you didn't see me for the first twenty years of my life?'

'Exactly,' he said. 'I see your brain isn't filled with orange peel after all.'

The fifth time I met my father was very brief.

'I'd love to stay longer,' he said. 'But I've got a flight to catch.'

The sixth time I met my father I was wearing a 'Save the Gays' T-shirt.

'Is this where you tell me you're coming out?' he said.

'I just support the cause,' I said.

He ordered us drinks and we got drunk.

'I don't mind two guys wanting to fuck,' he said. 'But why do they always have to do the voice?'

'The voice?' I said.

'Yeah, the gay voice.'

I looked at him.

'Oh, you have to forgive me,' he said. 'I come from a different time. All this is new to me.'

The seventh time I met my father was at my graduation.

'Looking good,' he said to me. 'The cape becomes you.'

He asked people to take photos of us – me, my mother, and him. My mother spent the day looking at him, as if he were a song whose title she couldn't quite remember.

He took us out for dinner and we all got drunk.

That night he and my mother slept together again. I know this because he told me.

'In case you were wondering,' he said, over breakfast. 'The answer is yes. She does have a mole on her bum.'

He tore a croissant with his teeth.

The eighth time I met my father lasted the longest. He moved in with me and my mother.

'The family's like a face now,' he said, as I helped him carry in a leather couch from the van. 'Me and your mother are the eyes and you're just under us, you're the nose.'

'Nice,' I said. 'Very poetic.'

My mother was the happiest I'd ever seen her. She begun waking up before eight. She'd make us breakfast. She'd make dinner in the evenings. She would even pack us lunches for daytrips. Things were good and they were happy. They married in the summer and I walked my mother down the aisle. For the honeymoon, he took her to Italy – my mother's first time abroad in over forty years.

Of course, these stories are all lies. My father left when I was young and we do not speak much anymore. But sometimes, late at night especially, I like to imagine that things worked out a little different.

Frail Deeds

My father sits in a chair.

'Fascists, I am fascists.'

I bring him tea and he slaps my face.

'Tell me when this is all over,' he says. 'I'll bring my camera.'

The chair: old, decrepit, losing its memory.

My father: stationary, broken-springed, in need of repair or better still abandonment.

My sister, a parrot of a lady, takes issue with the way I treat our father.

'It's inhumane,' she says. 'Why give him so much tea?'

'Good for the bladder,' I tell her. 'Clears it out all the regular pissing.'

'KFC!' my father shouts. He's watching telly and he likes the adverts. He likes the chicken.

My sister brings him Burger King, McDonalds, Pizza Hut and Dominos, but never KFC.

'If we give him what he wants, he'll have no reason to keep going,' she reasons.

The house: big, the rooms small. Many rooms. Fourteen rooms. The bathroom damp, signs of mould. Bits of soap stuck to the sink. Blotches of toothpaste on the silver taps.

A letter arrives. From a Roger Huberton. Claims to be our father, claims that the man in the chair is an imposter.

'Meet me outside Trecenydd chip shop,' he says. 'I will explain all.'

My sister and I discuss, make plans. Her husband, a policeman, runs checks. Huberton has a criminal record for assault, battery, fraud, and impostering.

We put the letter aside, keep feeding our father.

Father railing at my sister.

'Your mother never loved you,' he says. 'A mistake. And a regrettable one at that. Never got her figure back either.'

Sister feeds our father only flapjacks that day.

Collective memory of father once saying there was money hidden in the house. We are, financially speaking, stretched, and commence search for money. Sister's husband brings in experts. We insist that they do the operation at night, when father sleeps. Plan is troubled when father awakens to a young mustachioed man lifting a floorboard beside the piano. Father rails and hits young man with stick. Young man unconscious for a period. A few minutes perhaps, it's unclear.

We invent court proceedings, fake newspaper articles, show father footage of the young man taken from court down to jail.

'I can still catch them,' my father says. 'Still fight in me yet.'

More letters from Huberton. Tone is urgent, panicked. Says he has irreputable evidence — documents, photos, DNA samples — that proves he is our father. We put the letters aside, keep giving the man in the chair tea.

On a rare night away from father, I venture to the cinema. A French film, identity confusion, couples swapping lovers. Mildly amusing. Sit too close to the screen and this leads to difficulties reading the subtitles and following the action. Make note to sit further back next time.

Return to find my father sleeping.

Sister visits less regularly. I grow suspicious. Question her regards her motivations. Suspect she's been meeting with Huberton. Feeling: betrayal, sadness. A bit of intrigue. She denies this, says she has been spending time with her husband and her children. The children do not visit the house. Our father does not like children.

'Their hands are sticky,' he says. 'Their hands mess up the wallpaper and the tablecloths and the furniture.'

An evening, a few nights after argument with sister, the lights go out. Blackout. Father yells from the living room. I go to the hall, shine phone light onto the fuse box, flip the switch, but nothing. In the living room my father cries, shakes.

Electrician visits early next morning. A man, wearing blue overalls, thinning grey hair. Says the problem is complicated, will take some time to fix. Tells us to leave him to it. In the living room I give my father glasses of water and crackers. Noises from upstairs: woodpeckering bangs and thuds and the sound of duct tape continually being pulled and ripped. Father requests the Walkman, I hand him the headphones. Father sits, listening to dead men singing.

Electrician takes a long time. I go upstairs to check. My bedroom is empty, all the many spare rooms are empty. From my father's room the sound of duct tape. Enter to find man with thinning grey hair no longer wearing blue overalls. He is on the floor, taping photos and documents to a large pinboard. He looks up. He says: 'Will you just take a look?'

Sound of my father singing through the pipes, ceiling.

'You have prior charges for forgery and impostering,' I say. 'How can you be trusted?'

'Five minutes,' Huberton says. 'That's all I ask for.'

On the pinboard on the floor: photos of my mother, young, attractive. Some man — Huberton perhaps? — with his arm around her.

'Look at the documents,' he says.

I look. Receipts for clothes, coffee, dinners. Type on receipts faded, dates clear on two of them: April 14, 1972.

'So?' I say.

'I took your mother out for dinner that evening,' he says. 'She ordered a tomato soup for starters, lamb for the main, and apple pie and ice cream for dessert.'

'It doesn't say any of this on the receipts,' I say. I point to the board.

Huberton taps his head. 'It's all up here,' he says. 'I never forget a dinner.'

'Is this all you have?' I say. 'Food receipts and some photos?'

He reaches for his satchel. Takes out a wad of envelopes, a blue elastic band binding them together.

'From your mother,' he says. 'Twenty years' worth. Up until the very day she died.'

'Have you met with my sister?' I ask.

'Yes,' he says, handing me the letters. 'She's on my side now.'

Father calls for me. He is either thirsty or wants to change the cassette.

'One moment,' I say.

185

Downstairs my father sits serenely.

'Yes?' I say.

'Oh nothing,' he says. 'I just wanted to see if you were okay. You were gone an awful long time.'

Mao Oliver-Semenov

What's outside the box?

What do you mean your submission isn't about Wales?
We only accept submissions from Welsh residents or
Stories about Wales. Didn't you include just a little mention
Somewhere? A valley, or a mine or some hatred for the Tories?
So what you're saying is there's no Wales at all in your stories?

You mean it's not set in Wales? And there's no Welsh
connection?
Like a story about other places, that aren't Wales?
No Welsh characters? Like a story with other people in it
From other places? No mention of Cerys Matthews?
What do you mean your submission isn't about Wales?

How do you expect to get a grant? You don't?
You live outside of Wales? Outside of Wales? And
You want to write stories that don't even have
Some tenuous link to Wales? That are outside of Wales?
What do you mean you don't want to write about Wales?

You're a Welsh writer you say? But you're not in Wales?
And you don't live in Wales? And you don't want to
Write about Wales? You want to write about people
And places other than Wales? What do you mean exactly?
Do you mean you're not going to write about Wales?

Siôn Tomos Owen

God Bless 'merica

The guy next door was always working on his house. It was always hot and he was usually sweating, his forehead shining; his thick black beard must have made him even hotter. He'd tie his hair up by wrapping something around his head. He always did this. No matter how hot it was. His hand-drawn plans would be laid out on his dusty yard, held down by large stones on each corner. He had a small blanket under the olive tree where he'd take a break just after midday. He always kept a jug of water and a bowl next to the rug. He never drank it, even though it was probably thirsty work, he only ever washed with it.

He'd been building an extension at the back of his house for years. It was basically a porch with a frame that would house his son's room above it. But he insisted on these pillars instead of your standard four corner structure. 'Five pillars for my children,' he called them. He insisted that the foundations of these pillars would be the most important part. Obviously, since people would sit on the porch and if these pillars weren't stable then the whole tower would come crashing down on top of them.

I'd seen his son in the window a couple of times but never outside. He was like the character in that book at school, who always stays indoors and looks out of the window then comes out and attacks someone or saves a girl or something, I can't remember. I wave at him, sometimes he waves back. My dad would say that it was nice to see someone else who worked hard on something important like he did. I never understood how he saw it as 'important work.' I didn't see how it was any different to building model ships or gardening. The difference between my dad and the guy next door though, is I could sit and watch the guy next door working. I wasn't allowed anywhere near my dad's since it was locked in a specially sealed room in the basement. My dad told me to never ever go near it, especially when he wasn't there. This never happened since he was always down there anyway. It's kind of like a photographer's dark room only it's got its own light source there that runs off a separate back-up generator to the house. But my dad doesn't photograph things, He creates them.

He says it's his life's work. I know it's some kind of huge design project because of the work in the study. I'm allowed in the study, so I get to see the plans, but I don't really understand them. My Dad says I'll understand them soon, but he needs to finish the manual. Uncle Moe comes every week and he dictates the manual to him, cause I don't think dad's too good with words. He doesn't say much. He's more of an ideas guy. Uncle Moe brings his tablet and types it up. When it's done, Dad's gonna give it to…the patent office or something, I don't know.

Some of his drawings are crazy, man! My Dad's got one hell of an imagination, I'll give him that much. They're pretty freaking scary if they're built to scale. No wonder he doesn't want me to go down there. I'd probably have nightmares for a month. But to me they're just drawings. Like I said, I don't get to see the real thing. He says that they change all the time anyways. He says that by the time I'm old enough to be trusted, he'll probably have redesigned them into something new anyway. He's always editing and updating the designs, making them smaller or bigger, adding legs or wings, smaller noses, bigger tails etc. They're real detailed designs so I guess you've got to be pretty intelligent to understand them. But, 'I'll tell you when you're older' is all I ever get.

I think he threw himself into work because of my mom. It's complicated. I live with my dad because she's with another guy. There's no bad feeling or anything, Dad doesn't hate the guy she's with or anything. He works with his hands too, except he works with wood in a joinery. They just never really speak to each other. Dad only speaks to her through a mediator. He meets with Dad every few weeks. He makes me call him Mr. G but he only ever really speaks to dad.

My mom's pretty young so I don't think he likes to draw attention to it. It's legal and everything. It must be cause Dad's a stand-up guy. He always says she's the one, so he must care about her...she is pretty young though. I haven't really met her, which I know sounds weird. Living with a single dad who knows your mother but you can't see her or speak to her. He's not stopping me or anything, he just says I need to know some things first before I can move in with her, but I don't know when it'll happen. It's all got to be organised and things have to be sorted out first. I think the main reason it's taking so long is the paperwork. He always insists Mr. G 'sticks to the script,' so that mom'll understand everything that's going to happen.

I don't feel too bad about it because the way my dad talks about it, it'll be pretty exciting. He's contacted some guys from out of town to organise a barn party when I get there. I'm hoping it'll be like those crazy wild ones they have in college. Although he warned me that some of those guys can be animals. He said it'll be a party everyone will remember but at the time we gotta keep it quiet, so I think he's organising a silent disco. I worked out that he's booked my favourite singer to perform, Bad Ceaser & Amy D, cause I saw he'd written BC/AD on is calendar. I'm gonna freak when they come out but I'm gonna act all cool when it happens. I get presents too, which'll be a nice change since Dad doesn't believe in celebrating birthdays. But he said all that'll change.

I get kind of lonely cause Dad's always working and I don't really have any friends so when I finally met the kid next door who said he didn't have many either, it was pretty sweet to have something in common with someone.

I was outside practising my magic tricks. Dad makes me practise every day. He gets me books on sleight-of-hand, positive manipulation and some on hypnosis, but I mainly watch my Dynamo DVD on repeat. I watch David Copperfield too, but only cause I like his style.

When I was in the yard, I felt like someone was watching me. It's usually Dad, He's always watching, but this time it felt different. I looked across the yard and the kid was actually out of the house. I waved and he waved back, so I called him over. He was dressed like his dad and probably around my age, except he'd hit puberty early since he had funny little black fluff all around his face. But I couldn't really say anything, since I was rocking some lip fuzz myself and I'd tied my hair up in a top knot.

I spoke with him for a while. He was a little cagey at first and didn't really say much but when he started to loosen up, we had quite a bit in common. He told me he'd never met his mother either and he was going to be sent away soon to learn the language of his ancestors. He said his dad told him he'd need to learn his 'native tongue'. Neither of us knew any other bilingual kids in the neighbourhood, since we only ever really spoke to our dads. I told him mine could speak hundreds of languages but I'd only ever heard him speak one. He said his had told him there was only one true language and that's why he had to learn it. He didn't say what the one true language was but I suppose it wasn't American.

We spent the afternoon sat in the sun, shooting the breeze, looking at the clouds, picking out ones that looked like animals. We found fish, snakes, camels and followed tiny planes across the sky with our fingers. He said he could see a rabbit with a horn like a unicorn and a giant bird that looked like it was dropping bricks. I said I saw one of Dad's designs, the big one with the huge teeth and tiny arms. The kid had no idea what I was talking about. He said he could see a crocodile walking on its hind legs. I said it was pretty similar. I got my sketchpad out and drew it for him but by the time we looked back up, the cloud had changed again.

I asked if he wanted to draw something and gave him the pad. He took it and drew some pretty patterns.

'That's cool. What's it supposed to be?' I asked

'That's my language,' he said. 'That's how we write it.'

'What does it say?'

'They are friends one to another,' he said.

'That's nice,' I said, which made him smile properly for the first time. It completely changed his face. His eyes shone and he looked happy and it made me want to draw him.

'Hold that smile,' I said. 'I'm gonna draw you.'

'I don't know,' he said.

'Why not? Haven't you ever been drawn before?' I asked.

'There are some framed ones in the house from when I was younger. But I don't remember ever sitting for them...' he said.

'Well, what if I do you and you do me so then we can swap?' I offered.

He chewed the idea before finally nodding, but by then his face had gone back to being serious. So I told him a story to try to make him smile again.

I told him about the time my Dad threw a party before they moved in next door. Dad's not much of a party guy but this party, he invited everyone he knew. I saw more people at our house than ever before. It was bright and full, bursting with laughing and joking and singing. Everyone came dressed as all kinds of incredible birds and I got to stay up late to see everybody's costumes. They were amazing! I could have sworn they were real wings.

I'd never seen women at our house but there were more women at the party than I thought Dad even knew. They were the most beautiful women I had ever seen. The guys in the costumes were going nuts over them. I saw a few of them sneak out with one or two. Dad wasn't too happy when he found out that this was happening. I think he thought that since it was his party he could have first dibs or something. I was sent to bed 'cause it was late but I hid at the top of the stairs to watch. I could tell Dad was angry 'cause I could see his hand in his pocket and his forearm tensing while he was walking through the party. He keeps this thing in his pocket to squeeze to try to calm himself down. He calls it his wrath.

He was looking at this guy, Lou, who was strutting through the place like it was his party. Telling people to make themselves at home, pouring drinks and telling people to have a good time. When Dad finally found him, he went mad and threw his wrath at him and told everyone to get out and that the party was over.

By this time everyone was drunk and having such a good time they didn't want to leave, but some of them were so drunk that when Dad was trying to get them to leave they were falling everywhere. The front yard was littered with some whose costumes had fallen at funny angles. Some of them wouldn't leave so Dad went to get the hose and started hosing them down to try to sober them up. He kept shouting that water cleanses and they should look back at what they'd done and be ashamed of themselves.

After everyone had gone, the tap wouldn't close so he just stared at the water trickling out of the end of the hose until he was standing in this huge pool in his white bathrobe. He finally got it to turn off and then started picking up the shoes two by two and dropping them into the big square box he kept at the back of the house.

I could still hear them all talking loudly in the street around the front of the hose so I went to see what they were doing. All their white costumes were ruined but they didn't seem to care, they were too busy kissing and groping each other. Then this Lou guy says that if they wanted to carry on partying they could go to his basement apartment downtown. So they all started to follow him, their wings falling off as they staggered down the dark end of the street and all the feathers were all blowing off into the sky.

The kid must not have liked the story as much as I did 'cause he didn't smile long enough for me to draw him well so I did him as a cartoon instead. The one part he did seem interested in, though, was the women. He kept asking about them and what they looked like. But really weirdly, he kept asking if they were covered up but at the same time asking me if you could see their breasts. Like he was arguing with himself. One minute it seemed like he was disgusted in them and then he'd ask more questions about them. So I drew his cartoon with a thought bubble above his head full of women.

He looked shocked when I showed him. Then he asked if I could put more women in the bubble.

'I'll put as many as you like in,' I said, a little surprised.

'72?' he asked, his eyes wide in anticipation.

I laughed out loud.

'That's specific!' I said and we both started laughing.

We were both rolling around on the grass when his dad walked over to us.

'What are you laughing at?' he asked.

His son shot up immediately and stared at the floor.

'Nothing, we were just…talking,' he answered.

'What's that?' he demanded, pointing at the sketchpad by my feet.

'It's just my sketchpad, sir,' I said, trying to stand, clutching it to hide the drawings of the women.

'Let me see that,' he motioned for me to hand it over.

I hesitated but then gave him the pad.

He got all red in the face.

'Who is this?!' he yelled, jabbing his finger at the cartoon.

'It's just a drawing, sir,' I said. 'I drew it of your son.'

'Who do you think you are, drawing anyone you please?!' he shouted.

'I said he could keep it.' I turned to him. He stayed silent as he looked at me then back at his dad.

'I said you shouldn't do it,' he whispered.

'Oh, c'mon!' I protested. 'It's just a cartoon!'

'Don't be so insolent!' his dad shouted back.

'People have been drawing each other for years. What's the big deal?' I asked.

'Don't you ever do this type of thing again, do you hear me?!' he shouted.

Our back door swung open and my dad came out and strode towards us.

'What's going on here?' I didn't think he was home but I was glad he came out.

'Your son has been drawing my son,' he said, composing himself.

'Hey, it's nice to see you out of your room,' Dad said to the kid. 'Let me see that, son.'

I handed him my sketchpad and he started to flick through it. A smile spread across his face. He ruffled my hair and winked at me.

'Haha. He must be taking after me,' He said. 'These are good, son.'

I couldn't help but smile, even under the circumstances. He never usually praised anyone but himself.

'He's disrespecting my son by depicting him as a cartoon!' The man next door said.

'No I'm not. We were laughing about it. You saw us,' I exclaimed.

'You need to make sure that he doesn't keep offending us like this.'

'He's just expressing himself,' Dad said.

'This is *my* son, that one is *yours* and like I told you before…' he trailed off.

'Excuse me?' said Dad, glancing at me quickly. 'Don't finish that sentence.'

'I told you when we started this that we had very different opinions about how we wanted our sons to be brought up, Godfrey,' he said, hushed.

'Allan, you wanted to go out on your own and start your own thing. I understood and I was fine with that, but like I told you, I made my decision. You want to make your own, good luck to you but keep your ideas and opinions out of my backyard,' Dad hissed.

'This isn't *your* yard,' he growled back. 'This land was ours before we separated. Not yours and mine. We agreed to share the land. That's the only thing we could agree on!'

'Well, I've changed my mind,' said my dad, narrowing his eyes, his forearm tightening in his pocket.

The kid next door looked at me expecting me to know what they were talking about, but I had no idea. They seemed far more familiar with each other than they had ever let on.

The kid and I stared at each other nervously before turning back to our fathers. We both knew something was happening that would be an inevitable change in our lives.

They stared at each other for what seemed like a thousand, two thousand years.

Then Dad turned to me and said, 'Jesus, get your stuff. You're moving to your mother's.'

Epilogue

'America is the greatest nation on earth because of our history as a God-fearing nation. We were created as a Christian nation, and as such, we have adapted the teachings of both God and Jesus. In that way, Jesus IS American' – Christ_is_Lord – Jan 12 2013 – Topix.com

Gareth Smith

Desperation

As I wake on the floor, I see her coughing blood into the sink.

Her head is tilted over the patchy cream bowl, greasy hair pasted like rat tails against a bony back. She's topless, her emaciated body resembling a modern art display of stretched skin and bulging bone. There's an open wound at her side, puckered and black. As I watch, it begins to heal itself.

I hear another splatter of blood as I ease myself into a kneeling position against the tiles. We are in the poorly-lit bathroom of a fast food restaurant that closed several years ago. It has not been cleaned since.

'She's skinnier than I'm used to,' Angel says, pulling down her lower eyelid and watching the fleshy ball squirm. 'Probably anorexic.'

'She was a drug addict,' I reply, lifting myself up on sinewy knees with the aid of the sink. It creaks. 'We both were.'

Getting used to speech is always a challenge. The tongue is heavy and limp, a dead thing in the mouth. I try running it along teeth that are cold and distant.

'You look better than me,' she states, matter-of-factly, scraping her fingernail with dissatisfaction against yellowed teeth. 'I look like shit.'

I can't disagree. Her face has an equine quality: a long skull accentuated with high cheekbones and doleful eyes. It is a body already pushed to the limits by substance abuse, used up even before Angel got her hands on it. While I am similarly dishevelled, there is a certain charm to the unshaven jowl, sculpted nose and poignant hazel eyes. It would be difficult to ascertain whether I was homeless or modelling for an alternative fashion brand.

The odour of open flesh is gradually evaporating; the gaping holes in our sides slowly and painfully close. She smiles at me and I return the smile – we've done it again, we've survived. I hand her a stained navy cardigan which is thrown hurriedly around quivering shoulders.

'Let's get out of here.'

I close my eyes, knocked aside by a sudden wave of nausea. My fingers grip the sink bowl until they shine the same anaemic hue.

'Are you okay?'

'I'll be fine. It's just the last few…adjustments…'

My whole abdomen spasms and I am thrown over the sink, clogging it with thick, oily streams of darkened liquid. The hollow sound of retching echoes along the bathroom until I'm finished. I feel her fingers caressing my back.

'We really need to go upmarket for the next ones…'

Casually stepping over the withered corpses across the floor, Angel and I leave the room.

*

We are always on the move. That is the nature of our existence. Though we think it unlikely that our behaviour will ever attract serious attention – it's pretty difficult to catch murderers whose faces keep changing – we still cling to the quieter areas of the country. The 'arseholes of the world,' as

Angel lovingly refers to them. It has been roughly eighteen months since our time spent in the grimy bathroom and this means that change – fresh meat, if you will – is desperately needed.

We have arrived in Heldd, a small town in South Wales. From its Wikipedia page, I know it has a population of 19,000, the SA13 postcode and the remains of a Roman castle. We drove through endless motorway to get here and have parked up in the nearest square of Council-approved tarmac. Rain smears the windshield.

'Can't we just risk it in a big city next time?' she asks, leaving the car before she can hear my pessimistic response. I follow her, staring across at the town which cowers underneath a magnetic grey sky. I know from brief internet research that it has been an insignificant dot on the map for centuries, gaining a little prestige and a facelift under the Victorians. Many of the buildings have the dignified, humourless architecture of the era and the vague stench in the air suggests they are equally attached to its antiquated sewer system.

A middle-aged woman with a puffy face is jabbing angrily at the ticket machine.

'Bloody useless crap.' She slaps the side of it which, bizarrely, does the trick. A rectangular white tongue pokes from the slot. 'Three pound fifty – no wonder the shops are empty!'

She shuffles away. Angel and I exchange a shrug. We pay for our parking and head towards the high street. A banner above us proclaims 'Heldd Regeneration – Spring 2019' and the evidence of said regeneration is everywhere. Scaffolding circles most buildings like an unpleasant infection, barnacled to the Victorian fittings. Pavement is uprooted, grubby pipes laying criss-cross behind squares of red and white tape. Shop windows desperately exclaim 'We're still open' to streets of dwindling customers.

Angel walks a few steps ahead of me. Her voice is honeyed with sarcasm.

'Big changes, I'm sure...'

There are boards everywhere advertising what Heldd will look like after its refurbishment. As I don't know how it looked before, this means very little to me. It will apparently be full of laughing models and people pointing at trees. It will be a 'meeting of old and new – past and future coming together'. The clunky whirr of the pneumatic drill behind me suggests otherwise.

'I'm starving,' Angel states bluntly. I know that this apparently innocent sentence is tinged with a double-meaning. The meandering shoppers around us do not. 'Where's good to eat?'

'How should I know?' The high street doesn't seem to offer a lot food-wise, unless you feel like eating mobile phone contracts or payday loans. I see a red awning peeking from a narrow side street and make a beeline for it.

*

It's called 'Mam's Café' and is as twee and clichéd as that probably sounds. The tablecloths are plastic and patterned; the menu is written in chalk and hanging next to the door. Welsh slang has been stencilled across the walls; we are seated beneath 'Tidy'.

Angel ordered without even a glance at the waitress; she's too busy eyeing up prospective hosts. I, on the other hand, was paying attention. Our server is short and stocky, kind blue eyes smiling in a round face. Her dyed auburn hair has been pulled into a loose ponytail. It rests on her shoulder as she walks towards us.

'Ham baguette...tuna roll...'

The plates clank against the table. Angel raises the bread greedily towards her lips and our waitress begins walking away. I start talking before I realise what I'm doing.

'You're getting a facelift, then?'

She turns. 'Sorry?'

I point a thumb behind me. 'The town.'

'Oh, yeah…' She rolls her eyes. 'A fat lot of good that'll do.'

There are murmurs of agreement. 'The council keep throwing money that they haven't got at it. I'm sure it'll end wonderfully…'

The chorus of approval that greets this opinion is like radio interference in the background.

'And if it does work, it only gives the council an excuse to increase the overheads and then a chain store can buy us out.'

I break into a smile and she mirrors it. 'I'm well and truly on my soapbox now. I'm Ree.'

'I'm King and she's Angel.'

Angel lifts an uninterested hand. Ree's eyebrows rise but she's polite enough not to say anything. If she had met us only a few years back, 'Angel' was a muscly skin-head and 'King' a plump Asian woman. If you've ever seen a couple out in public and thought 'What the hell are they doing together?,' then chances are you were looking at us.

'Unusual names.'

Angel turns and looks her up and down. 'And what's Ree short for? Ree-ally needs to leave us alone?'

*

We are still in the café five hours later – it is raining and neither of us have any interest in shopping around Heldd. I pick at a jacket potato while she slurps a thick-shake. Despite Angel's brusque manner, Ree has returned to talk to us

202

several times throughout the day.

'How do you like waitressing?'

Ree sniggers from the side of her mouth. 'It's only temporary. I'll be out of here soon.'

I see the flash in Angel's tired eyes. *Hunger.*

'What about your family? They won't want you gone...' Angel's voice is lethargic but cheerful, almost drunken. 'They'll be worrying about you, little Ree.'

Ree shakes her head in fresh disgust. 'What family?'

'Oh no, have they passed away?' Angel: the Oscar winning actress.

'God no, they're alive and well. More's the pity. Money-grabbing dickheads.'

She begins to apologise for her bad language but I'm not paying attention. I'm looking at Angel, who cannot prevent herself from grinning ear-to-ear.

'Then make a break for it, sweetie.' She waves a frothy straw in front of Ree's face. 'Go for it. Take the risk. We did it, didn't we?'

I'm not sure who she's taunting more. I nod. 'Sometimes you have to take risks' is the most non-committal thing I can think to say.

'Like you said, there's nothing left here.' Angel continues in her heavy-handed rhetoric. 'You don't want to rot along with the town, do you?'

*

As soon as we're outside, I push Angel against the white-washed window of an empty shop. She hisses through clenched teeth.

'Get your hands off me.'

'Leave her alone.'

'She's perfect and you know it.'

'We're not touching her.'

Behind us, I hear bricks rain clumsily to the floor as they fall from the claw of a bulldozer.

'The uppity little waitress who already thinks she's too good for home…will anyone *really* be surprised when she disappears?'

I grip her wrists, digging my fingers into the veins. 'She's not for us. Understand?'

Angel delivers a swift kick to my crotch. My knees buckle and I puff sour air into her chest.

Her grin seems to linger even when her mouth is closed. 'I remember how much that hurts.'

*

I dream about the other people I've been: the skinny teenage girl with the peroxide hair, the balding businessman in his cheap and stained suit, the acne-ridden punk with the green Mohawk. I have worn their faces; I have walked in their feet. My present body will not last much longer; the darkening bruises that mark deterioration are already appearing along my legs and down my back.

Angel lies beside me in the cheap hotel room we have found. The welts run the length of her stomach, thick pockets of stretched, bloated skin. Her fingernails are beginning to pull away from the flesh and she pushes them back on with anxious precision.

'I've got less time left than I thought,' she says idly, holding a yellowed nail between two fingers. 'I'm giving us two days at the most.'

'I'm not sure about that…' I reply, knowing her to be right. 'Let's sleep on it.'

She thumps the headboard with her fists. 'Why are we wasting any more time? We need to go after Ree. That'll be one down and one to go.'

I close my eyes, inhaling a deep gulp of stale air-freshener. 'We'll find others.'

I can hear Angel shifting position, bending her elbow and resting on it to stare at me. 'Don't start getting sentimental. It's too late for that.'

I don't want to make eye contact. 'She's sweet, that's all. We can find someone else…'

'*Sweet* has not stopped us before. I'm sure plenty of the people we've taken have been *sweet*.' She delivers her final words as a warning. 'If you don't go after her then I will.'

*

Ree is walking towards me with a cup of tea in her hands. I awoke before Angel and headed straight for the café. She hadn't even finished pulling the chairs from their tables when the tinkling bell announced my arrival.

'The missus not here today?'

The cup hits the table and overflows a little. 'We're not a couple.'

Since that moment, we have talked almost non-stop. I know so much; I know *too* much. She has numerous step- and half- siblings, out of whom only two are spoken of with any affection. Jess is 'a little tomboy' and 'exactly like me at that age', while new-born baby Jake is 'so bloody gorgeous I could eat him'. She has begun several university courses and subsequently dropped out. She enjoys creative writing but doubts her talent. She took in a cat called 'Moomin' from a neglectful neighbour.

Her eyes flitter across to the clock. 'Jesus, we've been talking for ages!'

The café is still empty. Hammering and drilling provide a distant soundtrack.

'And you've got no intention of staying around to see the new Heldd?'

She exhales, sending a few stray strands of hair flying above her forehead. 'How different will it be from the old Heldd?'

The bell tinkles again. I know who it is without turning around.

'Leaving without me, honey?' Her braying laugh sends cold spots down my back. Her fingers graze my shoulder blade. 'And I find you flirting with our waitress...'

'I'm very professional; I'll have you know...' Ree says, with mock horror at the thought. 'Can I get you anything?'

'No. We'll be leaving any time now...'

As Angel passes to sit opposite me, she subtly lifts her hair to expose the side of her neck. It is a patch of crusted black, oozing slightly at the edges. I have the exact same marks all over my body. I can feel the cold air inside of them.

She mouths one word through cracked and pale lips. 'Now.'

There is almost perfect silence in the cafe, the lone intrusion being Ree's trainers as they clip-clop to the kitchen.

'We could just die,' I whisper suddenly, surprising myself. 'We could give into this and not take anyone else and just...just *die*, Angel.'

I study her emaciated body for a response. She laughs and coughs simultaneously.

'I've thought like you a few times over the years,' she replies, which is a far more balanced and rational response than I'd anticipated. 'I really have, King.'

'Then why don't we?'

'Because of the hunger...' Hearing her say the word out loud makes my stomach clench. I know what she's referring to immediately. 'I know that you feel it because I do too. That hunger. The hunger to survive and grow and...*occupy*. It's in me and it's in you. It's why we're going to survive and *she's* not...'

Ree is returning to us, jingling change in her hands. The hunger gnaws at me from the inside.

*

Driving away from Heldd was difficult. Angel is at the wheel. *She* is now a *he*: a homeless man that we saw hunched inside a doorway opposite our hotel. His age is difficult to ascertain but he has bloodshot eyes and a scraggly brown beard. He still smells of sweat and alcohol.

'We're going to need a new car,' Angel says casually, running tobacco-stained fingertips across his cheeks. 'This one is on the way out...'

He's been doing this since we left the town: pointless, brainless chit-chat. In an awful way, it's an act of compassion. He feels sorry for me and is trying to convey a message within the shell of those hollow words. We have experienced lifetime after lifetime of a change and have been each other's only point of consistency. I will always be with Angel and he will always be with me – until the day when we stop trying to survive.

'Do you think if the rest of them were like us that they'd do anything differently? Do you really?'

He tries to reach across and grab my hand – I pull away.

'Please, listen to me, King.'

I don't want to listen.

In the overhead mirror, Ree's blue eyes stare back at me. Her pale lips open and close as I command them, displaying two rows of straight, cream teeth. Almost subconsciously, I stroke her auburn hair and let it catch under my nails.

'You can't let guilt –' Angel begins, but I raise a hand to stop him.

'I know...this is what we have to do...'

I can't look into my own eyes.

I watch the road and the passing cars, another stretch on the journey that will last until the stink of desperation rears its head yet again.

Katherine Stansfield

The girls on the train

are laughing so hard they're bawling, broken
by it, might be sick – faces purple
in the joke, sweating their blather and stupid
with laughter and I wonder why
when they're getting off at Borth
for fuck's sake, that Twin Peaks
by the sea, and I hate them because
I've become this Arriva Trains Wales seat –
my early velour glory lost to coffee
stains and strange holes someone's
tried to glue closed and as I watch
the girls tumble to the platform
in a hot heap of themselves
and what they share I see at once
that my writing is the line to Barmouth:
poorly served, subject to frequent delays.

Rose Widlake

17

Because you couldn't go outside anymore, I tried to put bits of it in a box for you. The smell of warm Welsh cakes, salty seawater, green grass and spring flowers. Birdsong and the bustle of the city and the pinky clouds that soak up the last of the sun before dark. I carried them carefully from the car into your room on the ward.

'Look,' I said, lifting things out of the box one by one to show you. You look at me briefly and smile, but I know you're only humouring me. The morphine drive resting on your stomach beeps and delivers another dose.

'Shall I read to you? Paint your toenails?' I ask, and you dismiss the idea with a limp wave. You haven't read a word for weeks now. The sun is shining right on your face but you don't seem bothered. I go to close the curtains but you mumble in complaint so I stop fussing and perch myself at the end of the bed.

In the beginning, when you first got sick, I'd bring you books. Piles sat alongside your bed like bricks and you'd stay up all night reading, even though the nurses told you not to. You'd get through four in a week without trying. 'I'm so *bored*,' you'd say.

And all we talked about was books. Because who wants to talk about dying? We talked about heroes and villains, cowboys and skeletons. Poems and authors and happy endings. We didn't talk about the series of books you'd started that you wouldn't live to finish.

Every time I left you I'd pray for a miracle. On my way home in the car I'd sit with my fingers crossed, my hands tucked under my thighs as if I was pressing the luck into my skin. And every week I'd visit, you'd look that little bit smaller. And then I get the call to come and say goodbye and I'm here, sitting on your bed, and I'm not ready and none of it seems real.

I look at your belly – full to bursting with fluid and cancer and poison. I don't know what to say to make this better. You catch me staring and I look away, ashamed.

'Pregnant,' you say, with great effort, and I try and laugh but nothing comes out. I squeeze your foot instead. I don't let go.

'Remember when we were little and we all went camping? It was my dad, your dad, your brother and me. All you wanted to do was sit in the tent and have me read to you. You laid your head on my lap and I stroked your curly hair and read to you for hours. I felt so grown up, reading to my little cousin.'

You don't say anything. I'm not sure you heard me. Your eyes are too tired to look at one thing for too long and each time you open them they roll around the room. Each time you breathe something deep in your lungs rattles and I wonder if it hurts.

And I think, selfishly, that I want to keep you. I want to keep you right here, young lady. You're seventeen and you're not allowed to go. I'll build us a den out of books and we can hide from what's really happening. We can slip into a story and flit through worlds and plots until we find one we like, and then we can hide there forever. I'll write you into words so that little pieces of you exist in ink, on paper

211

that strangers will read. I want you to run and dance and cry and laugh and love and be again, because you didn't get to do it for long enough. I want the echo of you to be loud. But I don't say any of this. I am a storm of emotion and you are so tiny and quiet and still and my insides are burning cold just looking at you.

'I'll just sit here quietly,' I say.

A knock on the door – it's my dad telling me my time is up. How can it have gone so fast? In the corridor is a long line of people, all here for you.

'That's my cue, beautiful girl,' I say. 'You'll be exhausted after all these visitors!'

I can't say goodbye. I'm not brave enough. But you are. You are brave and better than me in a million ways.

'Bye Rosie,' you say, eyes opening and rolling forward to focus on me for just a second. I can't imagine the effort that took. I can't let go of your foot. And you smile, despite everything you are still smiling, and my god I love you for it.

Georgia Carys Williams

The Giving

He has no name,
gives away parts of himself,
beginning with blood.

Then it's apologetic sperm,
maudlin marrow
and now a kidney has run away
with his liver, curled up
with a clingy intestine.

Next, it's the gulping pancreas,
a lobe of the lung and
soon, he'll be speaking
without a voice,
breathing someone else's
breath.

He shaves away his hair,
bags and posts it,
then waters the balding bed.

He pastes wings back onto birds,
then sits at home, waiting

for a kiss to land, to perch,
to pedal
through his blood stream.

But people are wearing his hair
and laughing.
It's been fixed into wigs
and glued onto dolls.

His wrists ache,
with the pulse
that keeps going.
His children have no names.

Succubus Speaks

She does not want to weep in your dreams.
Let her sleep, wings a back-turned couple
spanning the humless sulk.

Fevered by beauty queens,
her hind-legs flee to filmic kink,
backpedal breath, then pause.

Succubus screams,
not to be blamed for ear drum's beat,
your bedding of frozen bird song
or her limbs like eels,
snakes without speech.

Succubus sees
time grow, slow ache tacking
to turning wings.
She looks at me, a blind shrike,
whispers,
disappears.

Your lids flicker, then freeze.
Did she sink into fatigue,
or has she only ceased to speak?

Terry Hetherington

Feathering

Like birds to a park's fountain,
they flock from the new estate
to this inn. Blind to the vagrant
hunched to the wall outside,
they chitter of fresh nest building,
holiday flight paths and the
vivacity of their bright fledglings.

Among the bar's bustle,
ties are constantly fingered,
dresses eyed and skirts smoothed.
Supping my drink, I watch
an old proletarian species
preening new plumage,
seeming not quite at ease.

From a room above,
heavy metal's muted thunk
shakes glasses on a shelf.

In Memory

It seems it was always during
blander moods over booze that
some new war would come growling
on air waves to hound you to
a fresh concern for people you
would never know.
Your mind, sniffing the stench of
power, vomited the suffering of
strangers, your words soured
by the taste, deepened your scowl
of indifference at the hearing of
some petty local woe.
The face of a starved child, wedged
between print, haunted you for weeks,
and you looked to the jaws of the
ultimate fiery beast and wondered,
when.
You hated our class's connivance, knew
(and sometimes envied) 'their contrived
emptiness,' but loved them for their innocence,
cursing the betrayal of their ragged honour.

I shall miss you Tom, our sober discussions
and our drunken nights among the gentleness
of hard men, and the loud women you held
in disdain and used with contempt when the
need became pressing.
Your mistrust of women was absolute.
This sole ambiguity hung on you like
a broken word.
How fiercely we argued,
your eyes rejecting my vision of woman
as the Saviour.
Wait for me in purgatory Tom,
we may resolve it there.

If I could speak with you now,
I would shout louder than the
violence of your demise.
So many easy ways, quiet exits from
this world gone mad with the science
we abhorred.
So why the gun good friend?
Did you hope its roar would drown out
the cry of mankind?
That cry was ever your anguish.
Did you think perhaps, that for that
last fraction of your life's run,
you would be allowed this final
noisome peace? But no, you must
have known that the law of ballistics
would deny you even this.

Notes On Contributors

Emily Blewitt has published poetry in *Poetry Wales*, *Furies*, *Cheval*, *Hinterland* and *Cadaverine*, and has work forthcoming in *Ambit*. She won the 2010 Cadaverine/ Unity Day Competition, and was highly commended in the 2014 Terry Hetherington Award. Emily participated in the 2015 Enemies/Gelynion project, and was a guest poet for Literature Wales/Seren's First Thursday event in February. She lives in Cardiff, where she is studying for a PhD in English Literature.

Aimee Bray is from the South Wales Valleys, but currently lives in Cardiff, studying English Literature in university. When she is not reading stories or analysing stories, she's writing her own. Her writing is greatly influenced by her interest in feminism and her Welsh identity.

Jenni Derrick is an English and History student at the University of Southampton. Having found and developed her passion for writing with the Neath Port Talbot Young Writers' Squad, Jenni has written poetry, screenplays and everything in-between. As well as developing her own writing, Jenni runs the University of Southampton Creative Writing Society. This is her second contribution to the Cheval anthology, having previously been published in *Cheval 7*.

Tom Gatehouse was born in London and grew up out in the Mid Wales countryside. In recent years he has lived in Buenos Aires, Madrid and Belo Horizonte, Brazil, where he currently works as a freelance journalist and translator. He is gradually compiling his first collection of poetry, as well as working on a longer piece of fiction which may or may not become his first novel.

Grace Gay is a recent English Literature and Creative Writing graduate from Aberystwyth University. Although she currently works in Agricultural and Biological Research, she is still a keen poet.

Eluned Gramich was born in Haverfordwest. She studied English at Oxford and Creative Writing at UEA, before moving to live and work in Japan on a Daiwa scholarship. She has recently translated a collection of German short stories into English, and is currently working on her first novel. She lives and works in Cardiff.

Natalie Ann Holborow is currently writer-in-residence at Dylan Thomas Birthplace. Born in (and still living in) Swansea, she is heavily involved with the local poetry scene and thinks the Gower is well tidy, like. When she is not busy writing, running or hosting her Mad As Birds poetry events, she is working as a teaching assistant at a primary school where she also teaches creative writing and is otherwise known as 'Missus Hall-de-Barrow.' She thus does not doubt the creativity of the children. Previously second prize winner in the Terry Hetherington Award, she was highly commended for the Hippocrates Prize and recently longlisted for the National Poetry Competition. Natalie's first poetry collection is due for publication in the near future.

Claire Houguez is an editor and marketing officer at Parthian Books. She is a graduate of Swansea Metropolitan University and Swansea University, where she received a Distinction in her Creative Writing MA. She is working towards a PhD with a fiction collection capturing the neo-burlesque revival – the research for which has become a bit clothes-off.

Molly Jamieson was commended in the Terry Hetherington Award 2014. Her work appears in *Cheval 6* and *7*. She has a degree in English Literature from Swansea University and lives in London, where she is studying for an MA at UCL.

Lucy Ann Jones is a nineteen-year-old prose and poetry writer originally from North Wales. She's currently studying at the University of Chester, because she thinks the city's cobbled streets and cute coffee shops are hiding something. She loves all things fantastical, surreal and experimental. You can find her @LucyAnnJo on Twitter, probably posting when she should be writing.

Tyler Keevil was born in Edmonton, raised in Vancouver, and moved to Wales in his mid-twenties. He is the author of two novels – *Fireball* and *The Drive* – and a collection of short fiction, *Burrard Inlet*. He writes both literary and genre fiction, and has received numerous awards for his writing, including the Wales Book of the Year People's Prize and the Writers' Trust of Canada Journey Prize. Among other things, Tyler has worked as a tree planter, shipyard labourer, and ice barge deckhand; he now lectures in Creative Writing at the University of Gloucestershire.

Anna Lewis' debut poetry collection, *Other Harbours*, was published in 2012. Her new pamphlet, *The Blue Cell*, is due out this year. Her poems and short stories have been published widely, and have won a number of awards including the Robin Reeves Prize, the Christopher Tower Prize and the Orange/*Harper's Bazaar* short story competition.

Richard Lewis was born in Swansea but has also lived in India, Africa and London. He has a degree in Creative Writing from the University of East London and had work included in *Cheval 6*. He lives and works in Swansea and writes when the sun goes down. He is a regular in the local open mic scene and is currently working on his first poetry collection, as well as a one-man play based on his experiences with mental health issues.

Lowri Llewelyn-Astley, 23, is from the exotic Isle of Anglesey and is currently studying for a Masters degree in Screenwriting at Liverpool John Moores University. Her current hobbies are fire dancing, yoga, burlesque and rock climbing.

Thomas Morris is from Caerphilly. His debut story collection, *We Don't Know What We're Doing*, will be published by Faber & Faber in August 2015. He lives in Dublin, where he edits *The Stinging Fly*.

Mao Oliver-Semenov was born in Cardiff, Wales, but doesn't write about Wales. Since ditching his career as a banking clerk in Wales, he has published words and poetry in a plethora of magazines, anthologies and journals, a few of which are outside of Wales. His memoir, *Sunbathing in Siberia: A Marriage of East and West in Post-Soviet Russia*, was released through Parthian in 2014. It isn't about Wales but is still quite good. His poetry collection, which also isn't about Wales, will be released through Parthian sometime in the near distant future. Mao spends his time lamenting his lost youth and wishing he still had hair like Richard Lewis Davies.

Nicole Payan is from the beautiful west coast of Canada and is currently studying for her MA in Forensic Linguistics in Cardiff. She has not studied creative writing, but has loved writing from a young age. She has taught herself, as she evolved from writing stories scrawled in crayon about bunnies, to drafting novels that may someday appear on the shelves of a bookstore.

David Schönthal grew up in an alpine village in Switzerland. He's got a degree in English and German Linguistics and Literature. He first came to Cardiff in 2009 on an exchange programme during his undergraduate studies. Ever since then, he has repeatedly been drawn back to Wales. He moved to Cardiff in 2013, and is planning on staying in his new home. He is currently studying for a PhD in English Language and Communication at Cardiff University. In his spare time, he enjoys reading, tap dancing, cooking, more reading, and much more. 'Cairn' is his first short story.

Gareth Smith is twenty-four and currently lives in Neath. He has recently completed an MA in English Literature at Cardiff University. He enjoys writing both prose and drama. His short play 'Flooded' was featured in a recent Neath Port Talbot scriptwriting competition, while another play 'Papers' won the Sherman Cymru's 40th Anniversary Scriptslam.

Luke Smith was born in Neath, West Glamorgan, in 1993. He won a scholarship to study English Literature at Cardiff University in 2012, where he is currently completing his degree. 'No More Bets Please' is his third published short story. He lives in Cardiff.

Katherine Stansfield is a poet and fiction writer. Her debut collection of poems, *Playing House*, was published by Seren in 2014. A recipient of a Literature Wales Published Writer's Bursary, she is currently at work on her second collection. Parthian published her first novel *The Visitor* in 2013; it went on to win the 2014 Holyer an Gof prize for fiction. You can find her on Twitter: @k_stansfield.

Rose Widlake is the inaugural winner of the Terry Hetherington Award, which she loves as she gets to pretend she's as good as the writers who won it after her. In the past she's worked for Parthian Books and Candy Jar Books, and she now works for a live music charity based in RWCMD. She writes on the train on the way to work, and is still working on her first book.

Daniel Williams graduated from Aberystwyth University in 2014 with a degree in English Literature and Creative Writing. He interns at Planet Magazine and edits the online publication Long Exposure, which features new writing, photography, and visual art, and explores the possible connections between them.

Georgia Carys Williams was born in Swansea. She won third prize at the Terry Hetherington Award in 2012 and 2014, was highly commended for the South Wales Short Story Competition 2012 and was shortlisted for the Swansea Life Young Writing Category of the Dylan Thomas Prize 2008. Whilst working on a PhD in Creative Writing at Swansea University, she writes for *Wales Arts Review*. She was shortlisted for *New Welsh Review*'s Flash in the Pen competition, and her work has appeared in *Rarebit*, *When young Dodos meet young Dragons* and most recently, in *Wales Arts Review*'s *A Fictional Map of Wales* series. Her debut short story collection, *Second-hand Rain*, was published by Parthian in autumn 2014.

Yorkshire-born Jessica Winterton originally trained in theatre. She has worked as an actress and backstage worker for companies, such as Sheffield Theatres and the BBC, since graduating in 2008. 2012 saw her return to university to study creative writing, where 'The Oozlum Bird' first reared its head. Her poem, 'Black Heart; Dead Heart,' was also published in early 2015. Jessica's ambition is to combine her creative experience and write for print, stage and screen.

Liz Wride gained her PhD in Dramatic Writing from Swansea University in 2012. 'Welsh Dragons' is her third appearance in *Cheval*, and her short plays have previously featured in *The Swansea Review*. In 2014, her Dylan Thomas Centenary play, *No. 5 Cwmdonkin Drive*, appeared at the Lost Theatre's thirtieth One Act Festival, Welsh Fargo Stage Company's On the Edge, and Swansea University's Being Human Festival. The play had its final performance of 2014 at the Dylan Thomas Birthplace.

POETRY

Washing My Hair With Nettles

Emilia Ivancu

The Shape of a Forest

Jemma L. King

ALL THE PLACES WE LIVED

RICHARD OWAIN ROBERTS

Tattoo on Crow Street

Kate Noakes

CHEVAL

PARTHIAN

SECOND-HAND RAIN

SHORT STORIES